I0536232

# SOMETHING ELSE

British writer Robert J, Tilley has been a distinguished—if infrequent—contributor to leading science fiction magazines on both sides of the Atlantic, most notably *The Magazine of Fantasy & Science Fiction* in the USA, and *New Worlds* in the UK. Gathered together for the first time are eight of his very best stories:

Title story **SOMETHING ELSE**, deservedly anthologized as a Best of the Year selection by Judith Merrill, is a lyrical but ultimately tragic take on Man's first contact with an alien life form.

**WILLIE'S BLUES,** a unique slant on time travel, was similarly recognized by Donald Wollheim for one of his World's Best SF of the Year selections.

Plus six other masterly tales, including an entirely new story, **MEDICAL PRACTICE!**

# ALSO BY ROBERT J. TILLEY

*The Dark Corners: Fantastic Crime Stories*

# SOMETHING ELSE

*The Best Science Fiction Stories of*

## ROBERT J. TILLEY

**WILDSIDE PRESS**

Copyright © 2015 by Robert J. Tilley.

Published by Wildside Press LLC.
www.wildsidebooks.com

These stories were previously published as follows, and are reprinted by permission of the author and his agent, Cosmos literary Agency.

"Something Else" was first published in *Fantasy and Science Fiction* for October 1965. Copyright © 1965 by Robert J. Tilley.

"Medical Practice" is original to this collection; copyright © 2015 by Robert J. Tilley.

"Choice" was first published in *Fantasy and Science Fiction* for January 1972. Copyright © 1972 by Robert J. Tilley.

"Music Soothes the Frooby" was first published in *Authentic Science Fiction* #78 in 1957. Copyright © 1957 by Robert J. Tilley.

"Willie's Blues" was first published in *Fantasy and Science Fiction* for May 1972 Copyright © 1972 by Robert J. Tilley.

"Attack of the Hiccups" was first published in the August 1861 issue of the house magazine of the *South Western Electricity Board*. Copyright © 1961 by Robert J. Tilley.

"Outsider" was first published in *Fantasy and Science Fiction* for January 1982. Copyright © 1982 by Robert J. Tilley.

"Reason" was first published in *New Worlds Science Fiction* #101 December 1960. Copyright © 1960 by Robert J. Tilley.

# CONTENTS

# SOMETHING ELSE

The equatorial region of the planet that the *Cosmos Queen* crashed on was liberally decorated with mountains, one of which it missed by a relative hairsbreadth before disintegrating noisily in a wide clearing that separated the forest from its stolid granite foot. The dust and wreckage took some time to settle, and it was several minutes after that that Dr. Sidney Williams, having surmised correctly that he was the sole survivor, emerged from the only section of the ship that had remained in one piece. He gazed forlornly at the alien landscape.

Locally, this consisted of multi-colored and highly attractive flora, backed by a picturesquely purple range of hills. Dr. Williams shuddered, hastily turned his back, and rooted feverishly among the bits and pieces until he found the sub-wave transmitter, a tangle of wires and dented casing that even his inexperienced eye told him was out of order. He kicked it, yelped, then limped across to a seat that projected miraculously upright among the debris. Slumped on it, he glowered at the landscape again.

He mistrusted nature in the raw. His first experience of its treachery had included being stung by a wasp, blundering innocently into a bed of nettles and being chased by a cow. The result of this encounter, a supposed treat that had been provided by his parents when he was six years old, had been to instill a deep loathing of all things green and insect-ridden. Concrete, plastic and the metallic hubbub of urban existence formed his natural habitat, and he was unhappy away from it. The travelling necessitated by his lecturing chores was a nuisance, but he simply stuffed himself with tranquillizers and kept his eyes firmly closed most of the time between cities.

His undertaking of a tour of the Alphard system had been occasioned by sheer financial necessity. Unrelenting pressure from his wife for the benefits to be derived from a further step up the professional and social scale, coupled with the recent unearthing in Singapore of a reputedly complete collection of the prolific Fletcher Henderson band's original 78-rpm recordings for which a mere cr. 5000 was being asked, had coincided with the offer from the Department of Cultural History (Colonial Division). Following reassurances that accidents were nowadays virtually unheard of and that unlimited sedation facilities were available, he signed the agreement with a shaking hand, packed his personal belongings and equipment and left.

The ship hadn't even got halfway to its destination. Due to some virtually unheard of mechanical mishap, they had been forced back into normal space on the outskirts of a small and obscure planetary system, short of fuel and in dire need of emergency repairs. It had been decided that these could be tackled more effectively on the ground, an unfortunate choice in view of the resultant situation.

Dr. Williams got up and wandered about the wreckage, kicking bits out of the way as he went. He didn't know whether to cut his throat then or wait until later, but in the meantime he didn't want to sit looking at the surroundings any longer than he had to. They both depressed and terrified him. He could feel the ominous proximity of greenery and smell its undisguised, unfiltered presence, hear its gentle stirring and rustling at the perimeter of the clearing, see its fragmentary movement from the corner of his eye as he moved, head down, among the forlorn remains of the ship.

What did it conceal? Life? It had to, he supposed. What sort of life? Peaceful? Threatening? A timid, herbivorous creature that was shyly concealing itself, or a prowling, slavering carnivore that watched him leeringly from the green darkness, savoring his obvious defenselessness, waiting only until his fear was sweet enough in its nostrils and then emerging to take him in its claws (tentacles?), preparatory to rending and devouring him…

He swallowed, and looked around for something sharp. A mustard-colored, familiar shape caught his eye, protruding from beneath a crumpled section of paneling.

Dr. Williams croaked an exclamation of relief, partially occasioned by the reorientation gained from finding something familiar and also because it appeared at first glance to be undamaged. He dropped to his knees and eased the paneling to one side, his mouth dry with excitement, crooning softly and trying to keep his hands steady.

The case itself was thick with dust, but intact. The contents, though— He swallowed again. He wasn't worried overmuch about his clarinet, snugly cushioned on all sides in its special compartment, and it was doubtful that anything had happened to the spools themselves, but their playing apparatus was another matter. Although it was almost completely transistorized it inevitably contained a minimal number of moving parts, and despite their being made to withstand moderately rough handling they had recently been subjected to rather more than they could be reasonably expected to survive.

He unlocked the lid and opened it. Excellent insulation had ensured that the contents had remained firmly in place, but that in itself was no guarantee against havoc having been wreaked at any one of several vital points. He licked his lips, said a brief silent prayer, and eased the machine up and out of the box.

Nothing tinkled. He held his breath, and shook it by his ear, very gently. Still nothing. Dr. Williams placed it on the ground, and stared at it hopefully.

As far as he could tell without actually trying it, it was undamaged. Had he been a man of mechanical aptitude, Dr. Williams would no doubt have carried out at least a cursory inspection as a precautionary measure before switching it on, but he was not. All he knew about its workings was that it was mercifully battery operated and that it carried a two-year guarantee covering mechanical failure.

He wondered how many million miles away the nearest authorized repair agency was, and laughed, hysterically. If the machine was broken, it at least meant that further procrastination regarding his future would be quite pointless. Operative, it could at least save him from going insane as long as the batteries lasted (the case held several spares); also, it would almost certainly distract any marauding locals, if not exactly deter them. It was also possible, he was reluctantly forced to concede, that it would actually attract them, but that was a chance he would simply have to take. With the solace that he could derive from it, life would be tolerable for at least a brief while; without it, unthinkable.

With a fixed and slightly demented smile on his face, Dr. Williams picked out a spool at random, fitted it, and pressed the ON button. There was a click, a faint whisper of irremovable surface wear from the original recording that he had always found an endearingly essential part of the performance, and Duke Ellington's *Ko Ko* racketed into the stillness of the alien afternoon.

Dr. Williams sat cross-legged in front of the machine and laughed, deliriously and uncontrollably. Eyes closed, he immersed himself thankfully in the brassily percussive clamor that now drove back his darkly threatening surroundings, warming himself at the blessed fire of its familiarity. He roared ecstatic encouragement to the ensemble, whooped maniacally at the brief solo passages, and accompanied the final chorus with frenzied palm-slapping of his knees.

The performance crashed to a close, but Dr. Williams' cackling laugh still held the sombre clutter of the forest at bay as he switched off the machine with a triumphant forefinger and sprawled back among the debris. He had been spared. It meant only a brief respite, it was true; weeks, a month or two possibly, but with the pick of his life's researching to sustain him, his final days would be made tolerable, perhaps in a bitter-sweet way even happy. He would smother his loneliness with the greatest performances of the archaic musical form that he loved and which had been his life's work, seeking out each nuance, each subtle harmonic and rhythmic coloration, so that when the time came, when the batteries were finally exhausted, then he would take his leave smilingly and with a full heart, grateful for the opportunity that Fate had seen fit to—

Some distance away, the opening bars of Duke Ellington's *Ko Ko* grunted springily into being beyond the muffling barrier of the trees.

Dr. Williams leaped to his feet, a galvanized reflex that toppled him again immediately, as his legs were still crossed. Slightly stunned by his fall, he sprawled amid the wreckage, listening with a mixture of disbelief, puzzlement and sheer terror to the unmistakable (and yet oddly different) Ellingtonian voicing of brass and reeds that blared from the surrounding forest.

Despite his confusion, a small corner of Dr. Williams' mind analytically considered the possible causes of this phenomenon. His initial wild guess, that the construction of the local terrain produced some sort of freak echo effect, was hastily rejected. He was no geologist, but he was pretty certain that an echo that took approximately four minutes to become activated was quite beyond credence.

That seemed to leave two possibilities, the first of which was tenuous to the point of invisibility, the second simply distasteful. Either (1) another castaway such as himself, coincidentally equipped with identical machinery and recordings, had chosen to respond in kind upon hearing Dr. Williams' announcement of his presence, or (2) he was already crazy.

The music, he realized, was becoming louder. It was now accompanied by other sounds—the crashing of displaced undergrowth, a muffled thunder that could have been the tread of heavy feet. He felt the ground vibrate beneath him, a gigantic pulse-beat that was, he was suddenly and sickly aware, in rhythmic sympathy with the performance, matching perfectly the churning swing of guitar, bass and drums. Giddily, he pushed himself to his feet. Whatever it was, delusion or nightmare reality, he had to get away.

He bundled the machine back into its container, and glared wildly around him. An opening the size of a manhole cover showed blackly at the foot of the nearby cliff. Without pausing to consider that it might be inhabited, Dr. Williams lurchingly covered the fifty yards that separated him from it and dived inside.

It was a small, round cave, little bigger than a telephone booth, and mercifully empty. He huddled as far back from the entrance as he could, clutching the machine protectively in front of him, and peered, squinting, out into the clearing.

Beyond the wreckage of the ship, he saw the greenery part. To the accompaniment of shouting trumpets and thrusting saxophones, a figure emerged into the open. It was approximately the size of a full-grown elephant, bright cerise, and the upper part of its unpleasantly lumpy body was surrounded by a sinuously weaving pattern of tendrils that ended in fringed, cup-like openings. It was apparently headless, but two eyes, nostrils and a generous mouth were visible behind the threshing fronds. Four squat legs supported its enormous bulk, each the diameter of a fair sized tree.

It was rather, the sweating Dr. Williams concluded, like a cross between an outsized potato sack and an octopus, but whatever it was one thing was abundantly and deafeningly certain. It was the source of the music that now rang about the clearing in unshielded, cacophonous triumph, uproarious accompaniment to the creature's ground-shaking gait.

It trotted cumbrously round the wreckage, blaring as it went. As it passed Dr. Williams' hiding place, it tendered a creditable imitation of the initial statement by double-bass, muscular strumming that came to an abrupt and sinister halt as it passed out of his sight.

He shrank into a near-fetal position as one of the cup-like objects thrust its way through the entrance. It hesitated in front of him, then pounced, an exuberant movement that strangely reminded the almost fainting Dr. Williams of a small dog that he had once owned.

The cup explored him, the individual serrations on its edge prodding and stroking like independents curious fingers. Another entered the cave and joined in the inspection. Their touch was warm, dry, and not unpleasant, and they gave off a mildly lemon-like odor.

After what seemed an eternity, they retreated. Dr. Williams steeled himself for the next move, fervently wishing that he'd cut his throat when he had the opportunity. None of this, of course, was real. He must still be on the ship, delirious—possibly even dying—from the effects of the crash. Perhaps they hadn't crashed at all. Perhaps this was simply some atrocious nightmare engendered by his fear of travel and its imagined consequences. The ingredients, after all, were all there; his lone survival, the grotesquely impossible musical performance and its equally ludicrous perpetrator that now lurked outside his place of shelter, his...

*Ko Ko* pumped its way into existence again, this time containing a distinctly alien added quality. Instead of its customary animal-like elation, it sounded positively plaintive.

Dr. Williams listened for a brief awestruck period, then smeared the sweat from his eyes with a wobbling hand and tried to think.

Accepting purely for the sake of argument that the situation was real, what for pity's sake *was* the creature that now sat outside the cave making noises like the long-dead Duke Ellington band in full cry? He laboriously reviewed its actions, trying to build up some sort of composite picture that would give him a clue as to its nature and purpose.

The conclusions that he eventually drew, while outside the fifth straight rendition of *Ko Ko* thundered towards its conclusion, were absurd but inescapable. Somehow, in some multidexterous way that was quite beyond his imagining, it was capable of memorizing or recording what it heard and then repeating it in minute detail, even to the extent of approximately simulating the individual timbres necessary to achieve the final collective sound. This was sheer lunacy, of course, but Dr. Williams doggedly faced up to the fact that on the present evidence there was no other possible explanation. Secondly, it was either quite young or relatively stupid. Its attitude was clearly that of a dog or small child that wanted to play, the unmistakably plaintive note now having taken on a whining quality that grated unpleasantly on his already highly strung nerves.

His experience of both dogs and children had been limited of late years, a situation largely dictated by his wife who had no interest in either, but he knew that both had a tendency to sulk when denied their immediate interest. Discipline, of course, was the correct treatment, but he couldn't see how he was going to apply any under the existing circumstances. All things considered, cooperation seemed the better part of valor, a decision aided by the fact that absence of anything that could be remotely construed as aggressive intent had at last permitted Dr. Williams' curiosity to at least partially overcome his fear.

He opened the container, placed the machine on the floor of the cave, selected and fitted another spool, and pressed the ON button again. *Potato Head Blues* by the Louis Armstrong Hot Seven clattered from the speaker, well-nigh deafening him until he made hasty adjustments to the controls. Beyond the cave entrance, he could detect signs of excited movement. A tentacle tip appeared, jigging solemnly, shortly to be joined by others.

Dr. Williams took a deep breath, said yet another silent but fervent prayer, and crawled outside with the machine blaring under one arm.

The greeting that he received, he had no doubt, was friendly. Tendrils patted, smoothed and tickled him from all angles, sometimes clumsily, but all with a marked absence of animosity. Dr. Williams clung grimly to the still performing machine and bore the buffeting with as much equanimity as he could muster, flinching only occasionally.

The music chirruped to a close, provoking obvious consternation and an abrupt halt to the amiably excited pawing. This recommenced, briefly, as the caustic virtuosity of Charlie Parker's saxophone scurried from the speaker, then ceased altogether as the creature carefully lowered itself to a squatting position, its tendrils now moving in gently bobbing patterns that made Dr. Williams think light-headedly of dancing flowers. Gingerly, and wearing a fatuously polite smile, he joined it on the ground, offering thanks for the apparently safe opportunity to do so before his legs gave way of their own accord.

The spool took some twenty minutes to run its course. During that time they were regaled by the thickly textured sonorities of Coleman Hawkins, a brace of roaring pieces from the Woody Herman and Count Basie bands, an Art Tatum solo and several sourly elated numbers by an Eddie Condon group. Apart from a cautiously twitching foot Dr. Williams sat motionless, eyeing his incredible companion and its movements with wary fascination. Occasionally and startlingly the creature would counterpoint the current ensemble or solo with a phrase of its own, intrusions that initially did little to aid the subsidence of Dr. Williams' state of tension, but which he eventually came to await with eager anticipation. These embellishments took a variety of forms, each displaying an astonishing degree of sympathy with the performance.

The final number on the spool commenced, a dryly dragging performance of the blues. With a certain stiff embarrassment, Dr. Williams got to his feet, returned to his former place of refuge, and procured the component parts of his clarinet. He assembled it with hands that now shook only slightly, religiously moistened the reed, then returned to sit in his former position.

He joined in cautiously at first, adding a muttered, almost apologetic embroidery to the trombone solo, inserting his phrases carefully between and around its familiar ruminations. Other instruments joined in for the final collective chorus, and Dr. Williams went with them, piping plaintive comments that were interspersed with the occasional squeak brought about by nervousness and lack of practice and listening with one eagerly attentive ear to the now more frequent and brassily stated interjections supplied by the extraordinary figure before him.

The performance sank to a muted close. There was a brief, solemn silence, and then the creature began to make music of its own, single-voiced and softly at first, but swelling gradually to a richly textured fortissimo; jagged, dissonant sounds that caused the hairs at the nape of Dr. Williams' neck to lift ecstatically and his foot to match its insistent pulse.

It was some minutes before he fully realized what was happening. The music contained passages that he found vaguely familiar, but recognition, when it came, still startled him. A chromatic passage that was nothing more nor less than pure Tatum or Hawkins would be followed immediately by the creature's own variations, spine-tingling patterns that meshed perfectly with the rambling yet oddly coherent structure of the music.

Dr. Williams became dimly aware that at some point in the proceedings he had joined in again, contributing strangely angular phrases that he would never normally have been capable of conceiving, let alone attempting to perform. He ducked and bobbed and weaved with the music, instinctively following the tantalizing zigzag of modulations, somehow seeking out the right note, the apt harmonic aside.

At long last, it faded and died. Dr. Williams twiddled a startlingly intervalled and totally fitting coda, then sat in deep reverie, inexpressibly content. The skies might fall, he could be stricken with some dread and unheard of disease that was beyond his curing, he might even suddenly find himself viewed in a rather more edible light by the odd and now silent and motionless figure that sat not eight feet away from him, but nothing could destroy the happiness that he felt at that moment. In the past he had added his not altogether unaccomplished embellishments to countless recorded performances, but absence of willing fellow participants had always ensured that these were solitary intrusions onto already familiar ground. Now, for the very first time, the crutch of foreknowledge had been removed, leaving him dependent entirely on his own imagination, his own abilities.

And it hadn't been half bad, Dr. Williams thought. He felt a muffled surge of vanity, then let it come jauntily through in all its unabashed swagger. No, by God, it hadn't been *half* bad.

He glanced briefly at the creature, placed his clarinet back in his mouth, tapped his foot briskly four times, then blew.

Some little time after that, the strains of an exuberant and quite unique performance of *Tea for Two* played by an extraordinary collection of instruments that included bassoon-like croaking and something that sounded vaguely like a plunger-muted sousaphone racketed raspingly through the slowly darkening forest.

Despite his occasional recourse to prayer in times of stress, Dr. Williams was not a religious man and correspondingly had little faith in miracles, but he couldn't help feeling that his finding himself in his present surroundings constituted something closely akin to such a happening. But whatever the cause, he existed in a place of earth and rock and water, bountifully equipped with fruit and vegetables that cautious experiment soon proved tastily edible, abundant shelter, a total absence of any other life-form larger than a rabbit, and its immediate region otherwise populated solely by himself and the brightly hued being that had become his constant companion and sharer of endless musical excursions that soon left him with a lip like iron and an instrumental technique that he had never dreamed could possibly be his.

There were minor inconveniences, it was true. Insects were frequently present in both variety and abundance, but while they were an undoubted nuisance, he was, oddly, never bitten. Also, it rained—not often, but torrentially when it did happen. Dr. Williams found these things moderately unpleasant, but readily acknowledged that they were a remarkably small price to pay when viewing the picture in toto.

During the early days of his relationship with the creature, understandably excited by what seemed to him to be the perfectly reasonable possibility of establishing verbal contact, he attempted simple conversational training, but it soon became apparent that his efforts in this direction were to be in vain. It obligingly aped his carefully enunciated phrases—always, disconcertingly, mimicking his own light baritone—but there it ended. It was plain that this activity was simply regarded as some inexplicable diversion on his own part which it was willing to humor, and Dr. Williams was forced to the reluctant conclusion that its own mode of communication took some entirely different course to that of his own species. Possibly it was telepathic, an achievement that still remained little more than a dream in the minds of men. But his disappointment was short-lived. Musically, they daily reached a degree of rapport that spoke effortlessly of universal feelings and reactions, an emotional link that invoked his own immediate responses and from which he derived enormous comfort.

If there was a happier man anywhere in the universe, Dr. Williams would have laughed with uproarious disbelief on being informed of his existence. He still found it beyond him to fully accept that his present circumstances were anything other than a dream, but since he was a thinking man and therefore one who had frequently pondered on the true nature of reality, he was not unduly perturbed.

Perhaps this was reality and the man-made clutter of plastic, steel and concrete that he had suddenly and astonishingly come to loathe was the dream, a nightmare peopled with uncaring, uncomprehending individuals with whom he had never really communicated and whose idly uniform acceptance of the multisensory exercises that now constituted their staple entertainment he scorned with the fervor of the true purist. Occasionally he thought about his wife, and shuddered. Was it possible that such a person really existed, that such a bizarre liaison had been formed! At such times he would hastily assemble his clarinet, and then immerse himself in a positive fury of invention that successfully, if only temporarily, dispelled such horrifying shadows.

The pattern of his new existence was soon formed. During the days they would wander through the placid confines of the forest, Dr. Williams engaged in desultory exploration, his companion plainly content to let itself be led by its new-found friend. Occasionally, they came across evidence of a civilization, oddly deserted machinery that lay rusting and overgrown in the green shadows, always without any hint of its nature or clue to its ownership. At such times the creature would lurk at a distance, its customary exuberance stilled, only returning when they moved on and the corroded enigma was well behind them. Once they came to a village, a bleakly regimented block of impractically pyramidal buildings that squatted silent and deserted among the encroaching fronds. Dr. Williams entered one, and found its walls and floor liberally decorated with huge and rusting shackles. They departed, hastily, his companion tooting its obvious relief and his own ethnological suspicions further confirmed by what he had seen.

The creature's amiable lack of intelligence, coupled with its particular musical capabilities, was the key. Clearly, it was a member, possibly the sole survivor, of a subject race—slaves and entertainers, the playthings of a technically advanced but cruel species who had, for reasons that would almost certainly remain unexplained (plague?), deserted them, fleeing the forests to seek the shelter and assistance to be found in their cities. Dr. Williams hoped with grim fervency that these were either several thousand miles away or preferably on another planet altogether.

Each evening, as they rested in the darkening shadows, he would produce the machine, solemnly select a spool, and for a while the brassy effervescence or sadly declamatory strains of jazz, performances that spanned the ninety brief years of its existence as an entity, would stir the stillness of the sleeping forest. Then, when the final blast or sigh had died and the rhythmic pulse was stilled, the recital would begin again, and he would listen, head bowed, to the patterns of simulated brass and reed that hummed and chortled in the darkness, marveling at the now hair-fine accuracy of the copy, yet always conscious of the minutely subtle differences that labeled it as such.

For Dr. Williams understood his chosen music well, and his knowledge that in its moments of greatness it became a highly personal means of statement he found both heartening and sad. It meant, simply, that when the last of the batteries had been used, access to the music in its true form would be gone forever. Yet might this not be, he reflected, in some ways for the best? He was living a new life in a new world, and nostalgia could all too easily imprison him in a cocoon of memories, only partially aware of the truths of his miraculously compatible existence.

Weeks later, a spool faltered for the last time. Sadly but firmly, as though unable to bear the death agonies of a dear friend. Dr. Williams pressed the switch, cutting Chuck Berry off in uncharacteristically faltering mid-solo. He packed machine and spools neatly in their case, and when morning came scooped a hole at the base of a tree and buried them. The creature stood some little distance away, respectfully silent, its posture one of sadness and commiseration. Dr. Williams marked the tree with the five lines of the stave, carefully carved the notations of the flatted third and fifth in the key of b flat, then turned and walked away without a backward glance.

The effects of his loss soon passed. It still echoed in their own musical forays, sudden glaring reminders of lifelong idols and favorite performances that he learned to accept with equanimity and use as harmonic springboards to creations of their own. Each passing day found him increasingly aware of the understanding that integrated their musical conception, something that had existed from the beginning but was now of an interweaving complexity beyond anything that he had ever remotely envisaged. The barrier between them, composed of space and environment, was shredding, and they were moving inexorably toward a blending of musical thought and tradition that he sensed would be the greater both for its fusion and the inevitable discarding of parts of both.

This hitherto untrod plateau was reached one sultry afternoon some weeks later. Dr. Williams lay beneath a tree at the edge of a large clearing, drowsily contemplating the profuse and picturesque greenery in the near distance, while his companion wandered close by, droning a pleasant but seemingly aimless pattern of sound that played softly and at first soothingly.

A sudden and unexpected modulation occurred, a tonal and harmonic obliquity that caused Dr. Williams to stiffen abruptly and twist his head towards the now still figure that faced him from the centre of the clearing. The creature sang on, sounds that built gradually to a complex of timbres that he had never heard before yet which flicked tantalizingly against his mind, stimulating areas of reaction that were contradictorily both new and hauntingly familiar. Something boiled sharply inside his consciousness and as suddenly subsided, an abruptly cleansing explosion that left him shaking with unfulfilled awareness.

He sat up, removed the sections of his clarinet from his haversack, and assembled them with a trancelike deliberateness. Still seated beneath the tree, he began to play, probing low-register adornments that added harmonic sinew to the bubbling search, shepherding the other's inventions firmly toward the ultimate cohesion that he knew had come at last, and suddenly, like an exultant shout, the pattern was resolved into a sustained sonic tapestry that rang about the clearing, dissolving their surroundings and the very ground beneath them; timeless, placeless sound that seemed to radiate out to the farthest reaches of infinity.

Eyes closed, Dr. Williams let his now unbidden fingers seek out the ingredients that were his contribution to this miracle, never faltering in their search, surely predestined in the unhesitating rightness of their choice. He soared and plummetted in a vast sea of sound of which he was an integral part, filled with a sense of completeness that he had never known or dreamed could possibly be. Time was without meaning, space a boundless vista that echoed the triumph of their empathy. Weeping and unresisting, Dr. Williams let himself be reborn.

Soft and distant at first, so faint that he at first accepted it as a not yet integrated part of this happening, an oddly discordant note infiltrated his awareness, a gradually swelling intrusion that bored implacably into this emotional narcosis. Vaguely, he wondered if he had suddenly become acceptable to the native insect population, perhaps about to pay a symbolic toll that marked his physical as well as spiritual acceptance into his new world. He flapped a temporarily unoccupied hand by his ear. The buzzing persisted, loudly now, a pointless, jarring obbligato to the music which flooded about him, its creator seemingly lost in an ecstasy of sound and movement that grew in intensity as it progressed.

His inability to ever fully accept the reality of his surroundings had been a natural precaution on Dr. Williams' part, an instinctively erected barrier against the possible presence of insanity that he had only lowered completely minutes before. Now, suddenly, as the dark pool of shadow swept across the clearing and the huge and writhing figure that faced him, it was as though it had snapped back into place of its own volition, insulating him, so that he watched what followed in a detached way, warily waiting for its completion before committing himself to accept it as fact.

The shadow passed on, yet somehow it had remained, a whispily fringed darkness that now dulled the customarily bright body of his friend. Dr. Williams watched stiffly as its movements accelerated explosively from a graceful weaving pattern to grotesque and terrifying frenzy. Simultaneously, the music dissolved into screaming clamor.

The creature's collapse was slow. To Dr. Williams' disbelieving eyes it seemed to shrink upon itself, movement that was blurred by the thickening haze of smoke around it and which now touched his nostrils, acrid and sickening. He watched its tendrils aimlessly collide and intertwine, still blaring their dissonant agony but weaker by the second, a dying fall of sound that slid jerkily down in deathly accompaniment to the movements of its maker.

Its final fall was punctuated by various unpleasant sounds. It lay before him, a charred and convulsively deflating thing that bubbled offensively at irregular intervals. Otherwise, it was quite silent.

From the corner of his eye, Dr. Williams saw other movement. He turned his head to watch the small scout ship that had just landed and disgorged two men who now made their way hurriedly towards him. As they passed the still smoking mound they produced weapons and fired them in its direction.

How pointless, he thought. Anyone can see that it's dead.

They reached him and assisted him to his feet, sudden movement that made him feel violently ill. He stared at them, serious faces above blue uniforms.

"We had a hell of a job finding you," one face said. "The automatic signal got through all right, so we didn't have any trouble with the coordinates, but this place is all trees. You must be best part of a hundred miles from the ship. Why didn't you stay close to it?" There was a pause. After a moment, the other face said, "It's lucky for you that you were out in the open when we did find you. We couldn't have happened along at a better time if we'd rehearsed it. What was that thing, anyway?"

Dr. Williams found that he was still unexpectedly holding his clarinet. He shook his head, focused by squinting, grasped it with both hands, and swung it like a club at the nearest face. There was a startled exclamation, a blur of movement, and he was thrown face down onto the ground. Someone straddled him, and he felt moist coldness dabbing on his arm.

"Poor guy," a panting voice said. "He must have really taken off. If anybody saved me from a thing like that, the last thing I'd do would be to try and brain them." There was a prick that he hardly felt, and the voice faded, abruptly.

And then Dr. Williams slept and dreamed dreams that were full of huge shadows and burning men in blue uniforms who screamed and sang mad songs while they danced and died. He watched their fuming gyrations critically, applauding as they disintegrated into ashes at his feet. Occasionally it seemed to him that they loomed close, smiling down at him and talking to him in soothing voices, and then he in turn would scream at them until they were momentarily snuffed out, reappearing through the diffusing pall of smoke, once more singing their tortured and incoherent songs and performing their burning dance against the darkness beyond.

When the ship reached Earth he was immediately rushed to a place where doctors and machines were waiting to seal off the nightmares forever behind impregnable doors, and after a time they succeeded. Under treatment, his experiences shrank and grew misty in his' mind until they finally winked feebly out, pushed firmly and efficiently beyond the boundaries of recall.

He still knew—because he was told—that he had been involved in an accident of some kind, but the doctors prudently fabricated a suitable story as to its supposed nature and whereabouts.

Knowledge of the truth was the key to memory and possible disaster, and the treatment was an expensive business that the insurance people were reluctant to pay for more than once per claimant. Consequently, he was encouraged to believe that he had been the victim of a piece of careless driving on the part of an unapprehended jetster, and was indignantly content to accept this as the cause of the blank spot that persisted in his mind. He was also reunited with his wife, whose tearful solicitude was quite genuine and which lasted for all of three weeks before being replaced by the verbal prodding that he somehow found rather less bearable now.

Following a period of convalescence, Dr. Williams resumed his professional activities, lecturing to bored or faintly amused audiences on campuses and in sparsely filled halls, only rarely encountering a flicker of genuine interest or understanding. He had grown accustomed to this a long time before, but now, at times, he somehow shared their apathy. The music still stirred him with its brassy melancholy, but there were occasions when it seemed that its vitals had been suddenly and inexplicably removed, leaving behind a thin and empty shell of sound that rang hollowly on his ear. When this happened, Dr. Williams would feel something that was inescapably buried inside him stir faintly, a dim and fading cadence that sounded far beyond his remembering but which briefly moved him to wonderment and an intangible longing.

And at night he would stare up at the sky, never knowing why, seeking something that he could not name among the distant and glittering stars, the dying echo of a song that had once (and only once) been sung, and which would never now be sung again.

# MEDICAL PRACTICE

Wallace Snell's aches and pains were perhaps best described as vigilant.

If the ones in his head, neck, chest, back, stomach, arms and legs were temporarily absent, he could always count on the twinge in his left big toe being present and conscientiously active. They were like a well-drilled platoon, at least one of them always ready to fill the breach, solemnly committed to the task of ensuring that his agony, terrifying in its implications, continued without pause.

For years he had tried to enlist the aid of the medical profession in combating this alarming state of affairs, but all doctors were fools, a fact of which he had more than ample proof. If asked for such information, Wallace Snell could have named forty-three so-called medical practitioners whose frequently impatient dismissal of his quite obviously serious condition made a hollow mockery of their professional qualifications.

One bright July morning, the pain in his head was very bad. It kicked and drummed like a roomful of clog dancers enthusiastically performing to the accompaniment of a large percussion band. When informed of its presence, his boss, another unfeeling buffoon, suggested that it had perhaps been invoked by eyestrain, the result of trying to decipher too many doctor's prescriptions, further adding that he would be obliged if the figures relating to the Marshall account were ready by four o'clock and not a moment later. Gritting his teeth, Wallace Snell staggered back to his desk and courageously resumed his duties.

By the time the bank closed, the pain was worse. The clog dancers had now been augmented by a herd of carelessly rampaging elephants, each one seemingly determined to outdo its companions as to the amount of damage that it could inflict.

Wallace Snell took another large dose of aspirin and blundered feebly out into the late afternoon sunshine, pondering his chances of making it to his apartment before his skull finally submitted to this combined assault and scattered its contents all over the surrounding landscape.

En route to his bus-stop, he passed a new office block. A metal nameplate, in some old way considerably brighter than those above and below it, caught his eye. Strangely drawn to this winking rectangle, Wallace Snell paused, lurched across the sidewalk, and read it.

'C.Q. Spang, M.D.' the sign said, further informing him that Dr. Spang was also a K.P.R.S., F.Z.A., P.P.M.T., W.R.O.M., G.B.M.S., and E.L.C.V.

Wallace Snell was impressed. Dr. Spang was the possessor of a list of qualifications that made his previous medical confidants read like the bunch of ignorant amateurs that they undoubtedly were. He entered the building, took the elevator to the seventh floor as directed, and was shortly in the presence of Dr. Spang.

Dr. Spang was, in fact, a Betelgeusian who had been despatched to Earth to complete his pre-graduation fieldwork there. Primitive planets such as our own had long served as ideal testing-grounds for young Betelgeusian interns, homo sapiens uniquely odd physical structure providing more than ample scope for initiative and experimentation. So far he had found himself restricted to little more than the role of lay-psychiatrist-cum-ear-syringer, but his hearts jostled excitedly with each other as Wallace Snell described his symptoms in generous detail.

Wallace Snell was reassured both by Dr. Spang's sympathetic attention and his appearance. Betelgeuslans normally resemble large, resilient rubber balls, but Dr. Spang had wisely taken the precaution of disguising himself as a kindly, grey-haired man with intelligent eyes.

"Interesting", Dr. Spang said, when Wallace Snell had finally ground to a halt. "Most interesting". He pinched his chin, and looked sombre. "You are obviously in a very advanced state of multi-decomposition".

"I am?" Wallace Snell cried, terrified. He'd known it was something of the sort all along, but this was the first time that anyone had had the intelligence to diagnose it correctly.

"Regrettably, yes," Dr. Spang said. "But do not despair. The advancement of medical science has been such that virtually nothing is beyond the capabilities of a suitably qualified person such as myself. Naturally, a case of this kind demands immediate multiple surgery—"

"Surgery?" Wallace Snell said. "Multiple?" He blanched.

"My dear sir", Dr. Spang said, patiently. "You can hardly expect me to effect the necessary repairs by injecting you with some non-existent wonder-serum, now, can you?" He smiled, dismissively. Such a serum existed, of course, but as well as being prohibitively expensive there was no call whatever for it in Wallace Snell's case. Besides, he was badly in need of some minor surgery practice, having barely scraped a C- in his last exams. "You have just listed a series of discomforts which plainly show that you are in need of drastic treatment from your follicles down to the soles of your feet. Rest assured, however, that this will be completely painless. Also, you have my personal guarantee that you will emerge from it all a new man." Dr. Spang was not without his sense of humour. He eyed Wallace Snell's doubtful expression keenly. "You remain sceptical? Which part of you is giving most discomfort at the present time?"

His head, Wallace Snell noted with thankful surprise, was better, but as always his left bit: toe was generating its customary persistent ache. He cautiously informed Dr. Spang of this.

"I see", Dr. Spang said, concealing his disappointment. He could have wished for something a little more challenging to begin with, like an arm or a leg, but these would come in good time. "Kindly remove your shoe and sock and lay on the couch". Wallace Snell did as he was told. Dr. Spang studied his foot, and rose, "Please remain where you are. I shall be with you in just a moment."

He retired to an inner roan, and sorted through his stock. He was a little short on toes, but a brief search unearthed a moderately good match. He took a small capsule from a cupboard, returned to the surgery, and rolled up Wallace Snell's left trouser-leg.

"The merest touch of anaesthetic…" Dr. Spang said, and sprinkled the contents of the capsule onto his patient's hairy calf. Wallace Snell's leg went pleasantly numb and an overwhelming desire to sleep came ewer him.

He succumbed, waking what seemed moments later—in fact, it was a little over ten minutes—to find Dr. Spang beaming benevolently down at him.

"How does it feel?"

Wallace Snell waggled his toes, experimentally. His big left toe felt fine, better, if truth be told, than it had ever felt before. He excitedly confided this good news to the doctor.

"Splendid," Dr Spang said, "if not exactly unexpected." He smiled again, kindly. "If you will excuse me for just one moment…" He removed the small container that mercifully concealed Wallace Snell's original and genuinely rheumatic toe, to the inner room, and returned. "Well, now. I hope that this little demonstration has convinced you that you have nothing to fear when the complete overhaul takes place—" He waved aside Wallace Snell's apprehensive queries regarding cost. "My dear sir, in a case such as yours, I consider it my humanitarian duty to act at once. Monetary considerations are of no consequence at such times, and delay could well prove fatal," His fingers twitched, hungrily. "Please remove all your clothing."

Wallace Snell did so, and was once again sedated into deep slumber. For the next hour and a half, Dr. Spang experimented happily, meticulously replacing a limb here, an organ there. The head proved rather difficult to match from his limited stock, but a little remoulding finally provided a reasonable facsimile. Dr. Spang transferred Wallace Snell's brain to its new home, removing the roots of his acute hypochondria in the process, checked all seams and joins, made one or two minor adjustments, and revived him.

"You will probably experience a little stiffness at first," Dr. Spang cautioned. "Otherwise, how do you feel?"

Wallace Snell felt in the blooming pink, and said as much. He pressed the meagre contents of his wallet on Dr. Spang, who finally condescended to take five dollars, then ushered him out with instructions to return in exactly two months' time for a checkup, carelessly omitting to ask for his name and address as he did so.

Wallace Snell departed, ate an enormous meal at an expensive restaurant, picked up a voluptuous redhead in a downtown bar, and spent the evening of his no longer pain-wracked life. His demeanour at the bank on the following morning was similarly uncharacteristically ebullient, causing first astonished then suspicious glances to be cast in his direction. At the end of the morning, the head-cashier approached him, his brow creased in a baffled frown.

"Now, look, Snell," Mr. Palfrey said. "I don't want you to think that I'm not pleased to see you obviously improved in health, but one of the stenographers tells me that when she met you in the corridor a while ago—" His eyes widened, and he staggered back, "Guards! Guards! Come and get this man! He's an imposter!"

This did, indeed, appear to be the case. At the subsequent thorough physical examination it was pointed out to the hotly protesting Wallace Snell that his eyes were now bright blue instead of grey, that his nose was wider than it should have been, his front teeth were no longer slightly decayed, and that the lobe of his right ear had mysteriously returned after a ten-year absence. He was also minus all other distinguishing marks that were recorded on his initial employment file, and his fingerprints didn't match, either.

His hysterical story about a doctor whose name he couldn't quite remember (Spring? Strong?) was investigated, but no doctor was resident in the building that he specified. Wallace Snell was sent for trial, charged with causing the disappearance of one Wallace Snell, employee at the Brinkman National Bank, and thereafter impersonating him with intent to rob or defraud. At the trail, the clumsy manner in which this had been done was widely commented on; the obvious physical disparities that must inevitably have been detected by those people accustomed to working closely with his victim, the completely out-of-character behaviour of the defendant at the time of his impersonation, etc., etc. The fate of the never-to-be-found Wallace Snell was also gloomily speculated on. Surely, the press coldly queried, despite the absence of a body the principal charge should have been one of murder?

Wallace Snell, steadfastly refusing to answer to any other name, was sentenced to twenty years imprisonment, and went to jail. There, one month after his interment, he quietly hanged himself with his pyjama jacket. In view of the impossibility of identification, the corresponding absence of relatives, and bearing in mind the crowded conditions to be found in the communal cemetery, his remains were cremated, an unfortunately chosen means of disposal as the material of which he was now largely composed exploded violently when subjected to a heat of 472 F. It did so on this occasion, creating a large area of devastation in the process.

Young Dr. Spang, having removed all evidence and memory of his brief presence on earth, had joyfully returned home on the same day that he had performed his mutually satisfactory surgery on Wallace Snell. He was received cordially and his specimens examined with interest. By all appearances, his teachers unhesitatingly agreed, he seemed to have performed a more than adequate job of dissection, but naturally his final marks depended on the skill with which he has reassembled his subject.

Some two months later, an examining committee accompanied Dr. Spang back to Earth in order to assess this point, but although they observed his previous accommodation for several days, nobody fitting Wallace Snell's description, it goes without saying, turned up. Their ensuing suspicions were confirmed when Dr. Spang reluctantly confessed that he had no idea of the name of the man in question, nor could he tell them where he might be found. The committee failed Dr. Spang for general incompetence, possible deception, misuse of materials provided, and not least, for wasting their time. After all, as it was aggrievedly pointed out at the hearing, thanks to his unprecedented and expensive tomfoolery their delayed return home had caused them to miss the start of the squalid manjudor-bumping season.

# CHOICE

"Fantastic," Richard Abley said when news of the Hertzog/Spannier team's success was made known to him by a wild-eyed Miss Wilkins. "Absolutely fantastic."

He wasn't a man given to exaggeration. The Hertzog/Spannier breakthrough was, in fact, the biggest thing since the invention of the baby.

Miss Wilkins babbled on while he tried to grapple with his own normally well-disciplined emotions. Her near hysterics were understandable, of course. Her fiancé of nine years duration, a stolid, balding, normally cautious man who worked for the local power-supply complex had carelessly electrocuted himself eighteen months ago, only two days after an actual wedding date had at long last been agreed upon. Now, thanks to Hertzog/Spannier, the guests could presumably once again start considering the questions of presents and personal ensembles.

"Changed?" babbled Miss Wilkins, "I mean, I'm *older* now." She collapsed into the chair on the far side of the desk, weeping.

"Now, now," soothed Richard Abley. He wondered, reluctantly, if he should go to her and pat her on the shoulder. In addition to being hysterical, Miss Wilkins had put on considerable weight since the death of her fiancé, and he disliked fleshy women. "After all, what are eighteen months out of a lifetime? You don't think John is going to let a thing like that make any difference to something that, um, he's waited for so long, surely? Of course not. Of course not." He said it firmly, dismissively. Miss Wilkins sobs lessened faintly. "Well," Richard Abley said, smiling kindly. "This is wonderful news for all of us, of course, Miss Wilkins, but there really are one or two things I should get clear before leaving this evening. I wonder if you'd mind getting out the McCutcheon file? And I believe Mr, Deny wanted a word with me about that man we interviewed yesterday afternoon, Mr. Clothier."

Despite the magnitude of the occasion, seven years of tidily devoted service prized Miss Wilkins out of the chair and into the outer office where the sound of shuffled envelopes was punctuated by an occasional sniff. Richard Abley rose, shut the door, and went back to his seat.

He stared at the desk top, a small, hard lump in his throat, thinking about his father.

Like Richard Abley, his father had been a tall, elegantly bony man with stiffly formal features and a small, squarish moustache. He, too, had worked in personnel management, at a firm very similar to the one which now employed his son.

Richard's choice of career had been in no way coincidental, nor had it stemmed from a reluctant sense of duty as is so often the case with professional continuity in families. His father was in personnel management; therefore personnel management had been the inevitable path that he himself should follow. If Charles Abley had been a deep-sea diver, Richard would have been irresistibly drawn to the ocean depths, happy to trail in the wake of such a precedent, neither conscious of nor embarrassed by the shadow-like sameness of his choice.

Like father, like son, was no careless generalization in the Abley family. In addition to these marked similarities in appearance, temperament, and selection of career, their affection, too, had been mutual. Charles, a widower since shortly after Richard's birth, had raised his son with pride and care, ensuring that his basic needs were never lacking; equally, in his methodical way, he had seen to it that industry and good behaviour were encouraged and duly rewarded. Richard's response to this treatment during his formative years had been to regard his father as a more than usually kindly and understanding deity; later, as his own understanding matured, he had come to appreciate that Charles Abley was, in fact, a rather unusual man whose patience and unruffled rationality were the exception among parents rather than the rule.

In a brutal and clearly insane world, these qualities seemed to Richard to be not only desirable but essential if an acceptable life was to be achieved. Correspondingly and perfectly contentedly, he followed what were, after all, the dictates of his own nature and, like his father before him, grew up to be a calm, rational, conscientious, systematic and good-natured man, this latter quality being not always evident in the rather rigid exterior that he presented to the outside world and stemming from a certain natural reserve also common to them both.

Despite the success of his own marriage, now in its eighth year, Richard had been stunned by the death of his father, a premature and abrupt demise at the relatively early age of fifty-nine. He had seemed in good health immediately prior to his blue-faced collapse, but as is often the case with people who have never previously experienced serious illness, his solitary brush with it had also been his last.

A little over a year now. Richard Abley stared fixedly at the desk top, dimly aware, of the moistness of his palms. It had been a lonely year, despite Margaret's genuine solicitude and her attempts to comfort him. When memories that simultaneously warmed and pained reared up in his mind.

But now it was over. At that moment, all over the world, people like him would be shedding their grief, rejoicing. For he that is dead will soon rise again, Richard thought humbly. The grave was about to surrender its grimly inevitable monopoly, and from it would step his father, to resume his natural span in a world that could clearly benefit from the example of his many admirable qualities.

\* \* \* \*

Despite the fact that Population Control Year VII had resulted in a reasonably satisfactory 5.04% overall reduction in the international birth rate, there were still too many people in a world the natural resources of which continued to thin at an alarming rate. The Hertzog/Spannier process was both cheap to set up and simple to operate, and to have it publicly available without some form of restriction to counterbalance its effects would have been like deliberately overloading a ship that was already perilously close to sinking from the weight of the cargo that it carried.

Argument raged, both among the religious community and at less elevated levels. The religious issue was immediately confused, some factions within its ranks holding the Hertzog/Spannier discoveries to be straightforward blasphemy, while others saw them as the ultimate vindication of certain Biblical claims. Other people concerned themselves with rather more down-to-earth issues, such as whether or not it was going to be either possible or practical to allow any sort of resurrection programme to be put into force at all. If it should be given the go-ahead, what sort of limitations should be imposed?

Should it be a selective program initially, restricted to people of proven stature—there were already small, largely elderly but highly vocal groups clamouring for the immediate return of John F. Kennedy, Winston Churchill and Gamal Abdel Nasser, among others—or would this provoke a dangerously violent reaction from a world population no longer in ignorance of its basic rights as human beings?

And just how much sense did it *really* make to bring people back from the grave? How far back in history could and should the program be extended? And even if the choice was restricted to the relatively recently demised, how many people already elderly and frail would be brought back, for instance? And what would happen when they died for a second time? Would they, or anybody else for that matter, be automatically ineligible for a third chance at life?

And what about animals; pets, famous racehorses? Were they to be excluded from such a program, and if so, on what grounds? Etc., etc., etc.

* * * *

It was almost six months before legislation was passed. The International Council's Advisory Group to study the question of resurrection as it would affect individuals, states and the word economy—A.R.I.S.E.—would have preferred considerably longer, but public clamour had become so vehement that a pilot program had to be quickly approved and brought into force to at least partially reduce the temperature generated by this understandably emotional issue. As the chairman of the Group wryly commented at their first meeting, resurrection, like a great many other discoveries on which numerous fingers had been burned, was yet another unwitting *fait accompli* as far as scientific research was concerned. The mere fact of its becoming public knowledge had set it on a course from which there was no turning back, for the time being, at least.

The best that cooler heads could hope for was to hold it sufficiently in check to ensure that the minimum amount of damage was done to the general social structure until such time as it became possible to make an accurate assessment based on experience.

The final prognosis was cautious, but moderately favourable. During the six months that legislation was being programed, a carefully selected cross-section of fifty-seven people had been returned from the grave. These ranged from a newly retired iron-foundry foreman who had suffered a fatal coronary only three months before, to a chiropodist who had been dead for a little over fifteen years. The foreman had readjusted extremely rapidly, the chiropodist markedly less so. The point was taken, the programme restricted accordingly. Bit by bit, fraction by agonizingly considered fraction, the original rough format was amended and extended, until at last it was reluctantly agreed that little more would be achieved until the weaknesses that it inevitably contained came to light through actual usage.

Richard Abley remained outwardly calm during this period. His wife, a small, dark, mercurial woman, had seemed stunned at the time of the Hertzog/Spannier revelations, a not uncommon reaction among his acquaintances, the majority of whose powers of self-control were considerably less than his own. Subsequently, during the period when the phenomenon and its possible consequences were being discussed at international level, like a great many other individuals they referred to it sparingly, reluctant to build up hopes that could well come to nothing should the makers of rules and policies decide that the results would be so disastrous as to be tantamount to racial suicide and therefore untenable. But in his heart, despite his own personal reservations about the wisdom of making such a facility generally available to a species as emotionally irrational as the human race, Richard never doubted that his father would live again, soon; that once again he would know the almost mystical experience of facing a reflection of himself as he would be a quarter of a century from now; still himself, but grey, a little lined, fractionally stooped; a reflection that he had believed to be gone, if not exactly for ever, at least for the better part of his own remaining life.

He was at the company squash court, freshly showered and combing his hair, on the evening that the announcement was made. There was a small crowd in the dressing room, some, like himself, excercised and preparing to leave, others in the process of disrobing. All froze to stillness as the transmission was relayed through the small P.A. speaker in a ceiling corner.

The basic laws governing the resurrection programme were to be relatively simple. To qualify, the resurrectee must have been dead no longer than ten years, under sixty years of age at the time of death and with no record of congenital illness. Habitual criminals, the mentally retarded, and victims of fatal accidents that had resulted in irreparable physical damage were automatically ineligible. One resurrection per family—the definition of which was both generous and detailed—would be permitted. All fertile members of families wishing to avail themselves of the service—it had turned out that an even larger number of people than anticipated had no desire whatever to see departed relatives brought back into existence—must undergo medically induced sterility for a period to be decided at the discretion of locally appointed Sterility Boards, extensions of the Population Control Service. Families in which pregnancy already existed and had reached a certain stage of development—three months marking the point of no return—would be ineligible for one: year after the actual birth. Amendments to existing abortion law were included to safeguard against a sudden increase of applications based on emotional ties with the past rather than reason.

Animals would be omitted for the time being, but consideration was still being given to the question. Subject to results proving satisfactory, the programme would be run on this basis for one year, but amendments might be brought in at any time that they were considered necessary. It would start in a further two months' time, and all applications would be dealt with alphabetically.

Applications would be dealt with alphabetically. Richard Abley relaxed, carefully containing the warm bubble of joy that swelled inside him, blessing the fortuity that had preserved him from being born into a family with a name like Zwort or Zukowski.

On the far side of the room, someone wept openly. Richard glanced between the hanging coats, recognizing the dark, bowed head of George Purcell of sales, framed by a brace of awkwardly consoling colleagues.

He resumed his combing, frowning sympathetically. Of course, George's mother. He recalled the circumstances of nine months before when the elder Mrs. Purcell had died, an event that had kept George Purcell away from the office for a fortnight and eventually returned him pale and red-eyed, a shadow that had only been restored to its former ebullient self at the time of the initial disclosure.

Asthma and heart disease, Richard remembered. He slipped his comb into its case and pocketed it. Poor George. Even if the late Mrs, Purcell had qualified in terms of age—which seemed doubtful—her medical history would have inevitably ruled her out. Whereas Charles Abley, mercifully, had had an untainted record of health and had just made it by the slender but irrevocable margin of one year.

He collected his belongings together, bade those in his vicinity a quiet goodnight, and left, tactfully using the exit on his side of the room.

His welcome when he walked into the apartment was not quite as he'd anticipated it. In his mind's eye, he'd had a vague picture of a scene that, without in any way being specific, nevertheless contained certain basic ingredients; an affectionate, understanding greeting from Margaret, the long-postponed discussion that was now no longer curtailed by uncertainty.

Margaret was there, but her greeting was somehow abstracted, slightly reminiscent of her reaction at the time of the initial announcement six months before. She patted his arm—an almost—absurd idea!—conciliatory gesture, and drifted to the kitchen to fetch his customary squash-evening snack.

Richard studied her retreating back, shrugged, and went into the bedroom to put his gear away. This, of course, was the trouble with emotional people. They always overreacted at times like these, unable to check the upsets to their digestive and respiratory systems that extreme excitement invariably caused.

Margaret was no fragile, swooning flower, but she was a person of deep, if somewhat erratic, feelings, passionately expressive at the moment of involvement and subsequently drained by the force of these readily evoked emotions.

He put away his things and went back to the living room. Margaret was there, sitting by the drawn drapes, her gaze directed abstractedly at the opposite wall.

His snack was on the coffee table. He lifted the cover, took a sandwich, and sank into his chair.

There was a short, odd silence.

Richard put his sandwich down again, unbitten.

"Darling, are you all right? You look a bit pale." Margaret grimaced slightly, not looking at him. "It is the news, I suppose?" Richard asked. "You've heard?"

She nodded.

"It seems to have upset you more than usual."

She laughed, dryly. "It's unusual news."

Richard said, "Yes, of course." He stood up and went across to her, smoothing the hair at the back of her head. "A stupid thing to say. I think I'm probably a bit light-headed myself. But when I think what it means—"

"What does it mean?"

He slowed his hand, genuinely puzzled. "How do you mean?"

Margaret said, "Not generally. To you, specifically."

"To me?"

Margaret said, almost fiercely, "You're answering questions with questions. What does it mean to you?"

He said, simply, "My father, of course. Charles."

She nodded, and moved forward, away from his hand.

He stared at her, then at his poised, inexplicably unwanted palm. He dropped it beside him.

"Look, Meg, I'm not really with you. Wasn't that the right answer? What did you expect me to say?"

"What you did say." She rose, went to the coffee table, picked up a cheese biscuit and nibbled at it. She made a face, and dropped the biscuit in the general direction of the plate, missing it. Grated cheese scattered on the tabletop. "Damn."

"Look," Richard said. He suddenly had the disoriented feeling of someone who has found himself quoting from the wrong script. Carefully, he thought his way back into what he hoped was the appropriate dialogue. "It isn't this legislation business at all, is that it? Something else? What—?"

"Oh, it's the legislation business, all right," Margaret said. She sat down, crossed her arms and leaned over them, staring broodingly down at the carpet. She looked somehow very distant.

Richard looked at her for a long, baffled moment. He cleared his throat, and said, "But what exactly—?"

"Exactly, specifically," Margaret said, "it's simply that all along you've assumed that if it ever did get through, your father would automatically get priority."

Richard stared at her, his insides abruptly cooling to refrigeration temperature.

Margaret's own parents had rarely provided subjects for discussion between them. He knew very little about them, in fact, simply that they had separated while Margaret was in her early teens and that both had subsequently died before he met her.

The few occasions when she had mentioned them had been unhappy ones, plainly clouded with bitterness, and Richard had never encouraged her to enlarge on what was obviously a source of distress as far as she was concerned.

Now, like thickening shadows from the past, still indistinguishable in detail but unbelievably menacing in their very facelessness, they entered the apartment and approached him.

It couldn't be true, Richard told himself. It was a reassurance that emitted a hollow, insubstantial whisper in his mind even as he formed it.

Margaret's relationship with his own father had been everything that could have been wished by all the parties concerned, surely?

Charles Abley had been extremely fond of Margaret, seeing her not only as an attractive woman who bore a certain resemblance to his dead wife, but also as the result of a possibly unconscious gesture on Richard's part, a token of gratitude in return for the sexually lonely years that had been so conscientiously spent on his own upbringing.

Margaret, in turn, seemed to have viewed Charles as an altogether admirable father-substitute, attractively overlaid with a strong resemblance to her husband, whom she openly adored.

The first six years of Richard's marriage had been the happiest period in his life, and he was convinced, in hers. Besides, she'd *said* that Charles—

Hadn't she?

He said, hoarsely, "But I thought that you—"

"You *assumed* that I," Margaret said. "In actual fact, we haven't *once* discussed this thing in specific terms. We haven't really talked about it at all. As far as you were concerned, it's been cut and dried from the start. Has it entered your head at all that I might want my mother back? Or my father? Has it occurred to you that a marriage originates with *two* families, not just your own?"

She turned her face away again, her mouth wrenched down at the corners, suddenly near tears.

Richard felt a rush of affection for her. Selfish, selfish imbecile, he thought, viewing himself with sudden and unaccustomed disgust. How could he have been so selfish? Of course she was right, every single word of what she'd said. Not that she'd *meant* all of them, of course. She was, quite correctly, reminding him that simply because she'd chosen to remain silent about her relationship with her own parents that was no reason for him to have automatically dismissed them as altogether unworthy of consideration.

But the point had been made now, and he must show her that he accepted the deserved reproof.

He went across the room and knelt beside her chair, patting her leg, then gently squeezing it.

"You're right, of course. I have been a bit of a pig, haven't I? But when you miss somebody as much as I miss Charles, you're apt to forget that there might have been other candidates."

He felt her leg stiffen. After a moment, she said, "Might have been?"

*"Were,"* he amended. "Once upon a time, I mean. When you were a kid, I expect you saw them very diff—" He broke off as she stood up, her suddenly vertical thigh knocking his hand to one side. Still biting down on the uncompleted word, he stared with genuine astonishment at her hunched back as she moved away from him.

She halted by the wall, and turned. Her face was tight and very bitter.

"You still don't understand, do you? What I'm saying, exactly, specifically, is that I want it to be my mother."

Above the sudden roaring in his ears, Richard Abley heard a high, plaintive voice, quite unlike his own.

"But you told me you didn't love your mother."

"How many children believe that about their parents? Most of them, if the truth were known." She glowered at him with continued bitterness. "Oh, stop looking at me as if I was swearing in church. Hasn't it ever dawned on you just how much of an exceptional exception your relationship with Charles was? Continuous love and respect between parent and child. Ridiculous."

She almost spat the word. "And hasn't it ever dawned on you that that was an aspect of your life that I envied like I'd never envied anything, anyone before? My God, do you realize just how lucky you *were,* having all those years with Charles?"

Richard steadied himself (he was actually *shaking!*) with difficulty. He rose sufficiently to seat himself on the chair that she had vacated, interlaced his vibrating hands and stared at her from beneath worriedly arrowed eyebrows.

"Look, let's get this absolutely straight. You're really serious? You're saying that you want your mother back instead of Charles?" He voiced the anguished cry that thundered inside his head like a berserk carillon. "Why?"

"I suppose I'm no different from most people," Margaret said. She turned and stood in profile, staring bleakly across the room. "I was too young to really understand my mother up to the time that she died. When you're a baby, you automatically depend on them and take what they say as gospel, but then you get older and it isn't so simple any more. They impose restrictions that you don't really understand, and unless they've got all the patience in the world, you end up fighting. In a way, they become your worst enemy. You actually begin to hate them.

"But then something happens, and all of a sudden they aren't there anymore, and you're confused because you really miss them."

In a clogged voice, Richard said, "What kind of a woman was she?"

"That's what I want to find out," Margaret said. Her expression was now tinged with a faint wistfulness, "I've got a vague idea, but I'm sure I'm wrong about a lot of things I *think* I remember about her. I do know she was blonde and bigger than I—bigger than I am since I grew up, I mean. My father was the small, dark one. He was also a dirty little rat, I learned a lot later. He'd played around all the time they'd been married, and he was a bit of a crook, too. Oh, he didn't rob banks, or anything like that. He was just another sneak that lives barely on the right side of the law, that sort." She stirred, frowned, and looked at the floor again.

"Mother had a pretty bad time of it all round. When they split up, she went to a rest home for a year and I went to live with an uncle and aunt, my mother's sister. I didn't see much of her after that, and *she* died about five months before you and I met. My father was killed in a car smash about eighteen months before that." She continued to stare at the floor, her face drawn and mutinous.

Richard looked down at his hands, detachedly observing the hair-fine tremor there. He felt quite abominably sick. After a long pause, he said, "And you feel she should get a second chance."

"Yes, I do. Don't you, under the circumstances? Now that it's possible?"

"I see your point, of course," Richard said. He had the ghastly sensation of undertaking the most dangerous journey of his life, of balancing precariously on a verbal tightrope from which he might slip at any time unless he exercised every single nuance of control of which he was capable.

"You say that after your people split up, you didn't actually see much of her. Why was that, exactly?"

"She didn't want to see me, I expect, I was always a lot like my father in looks, and I'd have reminded her of him. Something like that."

Richard said, thoughtfully, "Yes." He felt a minute improvement in his sense of balance. "I imagine it was something of the sort." He stood, wedged his hands in his trouser pockets, and took a turn around the chair. "But—" He paused, expelled air, shrugged slightly, "I mean, if that was how she felt about you then, why should she feel any different if she was to be brought back now?"

There was another lengthy, prickling silence.

Margaret said, in a thin voice, "Because circumstances are very different now."

"In what way particularly?"

"My father is dead, for one thing. He's been dead for eleven years. She'll be over him by now and she won't resent me like she used to."

"Darling, that's pure speculation," Richard said. "It's bound to be, isn't it? Look, you remember what Waker said, how he described it?"

Waker had been the subject of the initial Hertzog/Spannier breakthrough, a retired janitor who had been chosen purely on the basis of his appropriate name and who had subsequently made himself a small fortune from personal appearances and ghosted articles in the press.

"He said it was simply like waking up; that he hadn't been to heaven or hell or anywhere at all that he could remember. All the others have confirmed what he said, except for that crazy Barnes woman, of course. The churches got around that one by saying that obviously none of them would remember anything of the kind because they wouldn't be allowed to, but you see what I'm getting at? If it's just like waking up, then the memory of your father will be just as strong as it was when she died." He stopped, swallowing the impatience that seethed inside him, conscious that his voice had been steadily rising.

"You're working at this very hard," Margaret said. Her own voice was still thin, and for the first time since they had met he heard a note of pure hatred in it. Even at a moment like this it still shocked him.

"You're trying to convince me that if she did come back it wouldn't work, that we still wouldn't get on sufficiently well to make it worthwhile. What you don't understand is that the relationship itself isn't the really important thing. I'd want it to work, of course, but if it didn't that wouldn't mean it had all been a wasted opportunity."

"Of course it would."

"No, it wouldn't. When she found out that she had a second chance to straighten her life out—"

"How did she die?" Richard asked. He spoke coolly, suddenly sensing that a chink had shown briefly in her defences. God, he thought, amazed, is this really it? Fencing like a swordsman ruthlessly committed to win the duel at whatever cost? He saw the flicker of wretchedness cross her face, and pressed home his instinctive attack. "Natural causes?"

When Margaret spoke, her voice was very small. "She took pills."

"I see," Richard said. Overriding his pity, he felt a sense of tired triumph, as though the fight, although not actually over, had abruptly shown how it was to end. "Look, darling, why don't we have a drink and sit down and really talk this: thing out? We seem to have got off to a pretty bad start, and I don't think—"

"No."

"No, *what?*" Richard snapped. He was horrified to find that he abruptly had a furious desire to grab and shake her, something that had never, even faintly, entered his mind before. "You mean, no, you don't want a drink or no, you won't sit down and try to discuss it rationally?"

"How can we discuss it rationally? It's so completely basic, an instinctive, animal thing. We're fighting for our parents, both of us. Our reasons are completely different. I doubt that you even know what your real reasons *are*—but it's still—"

"Just a minute," Richard said. He was breathing heavily, conscious of the sudden heat inside him. "What do you mean about *real* reasons? You know what my reasons are, and there's nothing ambiguous about them. Yours, on the other hand, seem to me to be a straightforward examp—"

"Vanity," Margaret said. "Love of self. My God, haven't you ever realized just how much you and Charles used to use each other as a mirror—Charles to remind himself of what he was like when he was young, and you to reassure yourself that you wouldn't have gone to pieces when you were his age? It was all perfectly understandable, rather sweet in its way, but it was pure reciprocal narcissism." She stared back at his wounded, furious face, a pale shadow of sympathy showing in her eyes. "I do understand, I really do. It wasn't only that. You really did love him, I know. He was a good man, and I've missed him, too. But, don't you see, that's what makes it so unfair? He had a good life—"

Richard said, between his teeth, "What about my mother? *She* died, too, you know. And *he* loved her."

"I know," Margaret said. She was fretful now. "I *know* he did. But he had a few good years of marriage, and afterwards he had you. My mother didn't have either. Her marriage was sour from the beginning, and all she produced was me, a permanent reminder of my father. If I'd looked like her instead, perhaps she wouldn't—"

"She would," Richard said, brutally. His head roared with an emotional compound the like of which he'd never experienced in his life before: rage, frustration, and an insane desire to hurt. He showed his teeth in a near snarl. "Once a loser, always a loser. It's the pattern of that sort of person's life. It's inherent in their make-up, the kind of limitation that's beyond your control, something that they can't grow out of. They're stuck with it, no matter how many chances they get." He turned away from her pale, slack face.

"That's why it would be pointless to bring her back. I'm sorry for her, of course, sorry for you, but you know I'm right. If we were to throw away the one chance that we might get—" He was pacing like an animal now, taut, prowling steps that weaved blindly around the room.

"Don't you realize just how improbable this whole thing is? It can't last. There are so many things that could go wrong that they're bound to cancel it almost as soon as it gets started. And to *waste*—"

The warning bells of instinct clamoured suddenly inside him. He stopped, and spun to face her.

She was advancing on him with the brass poker, a useless relic that had provided decoration above their main thermal vent ever since moving into the apartment. Her face was ghastly, the bleached features of an animal. Hissing, she ran at him, raising the gleaming rod above her head.

He stepped sideways, snatched the poker from her with one hand, grabbed the front of her dress with the other. He jerked her to him, and then away, hurling her back across the room.

Her heel caught on a chair leg. She fell, heavily, her rigid neck striking the edge of the coffee table. The plate containing his supper jumped, scattering its contents. There was a second final flurry of movement as she rolled onto her side, facing the wall, her back arched towards him in a belated and pointless pose of defence.

Sounds still clamoured inside him, screams of horror and denial that shook him like a tree in a storm. He dropped the poker and went to her, kneeling beside her and pawing her with fearful hands, massaging the small, still breasts, seeking movement that he knew was no longer there.

After a time, he lifted her, carrying her to the bedroom and gently laying her on the bed. Holding one limp and still-cooling hand, he straightened and stood looking down at her, his face a stiff and tear-streaked mask of remorse.

He stood there for a long time, weeping and remembering.

Then, regretfully, Richard Abley made his choice.

# MUSIC SOOTHES THE THROOBY

Wainwright was tall, acid, and precise. His tailored grey uniform, normally a thing of glacier-smooth surfaces and razor-like creases, was crumpled beyond recognition. He wriggled uncomfortably in his seat, and scowled about him.

"I do wish," he said petulantly, "that the authorities could have found us something a little more suitable."

The cabin of the scout-ship was small. Under normal circumstances it held the customary three-man initial survey team comfortably, leaving just sufficient floor-space for what gear was considered strictly necessary. The present circumstances, however, required it to accommodate five men and a small mountain of equipment that seemed, considering the location of the ship, somewhat bizarre.

"Oops," said Sneider guardedly. He pushed a foot out in front of him, just in time to arrest the progress of the bass drum which was sliding heavily towards him, threatening to pin him to the wall. He kept his foot against it and eyed Wainwright speculatively. "I take it, major, that you've never done any band-work personally?"

"Never," said Wainwright shortly. With a smouldering eye he peered at the double bass that was wedged, precariously, alongside his seat. "I have a degree in alien cultures, and am considered a specialist in the lesser-known musical forms. My treatise on the thirteen-tone scale, initially discovered on Golek, is currently considered a standard work in civilized musical circles, I believe. That, however, you could hardly be expected to know."

Greer's face, just visible above the snare drum case, assumed a doleful expression. In a bored sort of way he poked his tongue out at the back of Wainwright's head.

Wainwright said: "What are your reasons for assuming my lack of experience in—what did you call it—band-work?"

He made it sound like a dirty word.

Sneider said, cheerfully: "What you'd call reaction to circumstances, I guess. On one-nighters you get used to sleeping in the next guy's pocket. Find yourself bedded down between a heap of music stands and a baritone-sax, you think nothing of it." He grinned. "That's the circuit for you."

"Not," said Wainwright, "for me." As far as his cramped position would allow, he shuddered. "An appalling existence, if what you say is true. I think you would hardly be inclined to disagree if I ventured the opinion that you are well rid of it."

"Never had it this good before," agreed Sneider. "Play your way round the universe and get five times the M.U. rate for it. I know guys who'd give their ears for it. What do you say, Tubs?"

"The very most," said Klein. He eased his thirteen stone back in his seat, and winked at Sneider. "All the comforts I never had at home. Couldn't be cooler."

"I realise," said Wainwright sourly, "that the monetary aspect is bound to have a certain appeal, but surely there are other, deeper satisfactions to be obtained from what you are doing? In your own, oddly discordant way, you are introducing these people to one of the most aesthetically satisfying of the arts. Your own particular type of musical interpretation, by virtue of its very simplicity and origin, has been found to invoke a far greater response among the uncivilized alien races than has that of the more serious kind. But, after all," said Wainwright sniffily, "these people are savages."

"Savages?" said Perkins. He poked his tongue from the corner of his mouth, dubiously, and cocked an eyebrow at Sneider. "It's a little late to carp, I know, but this is the first I heard…"

"Not," said Wainwright, "savages in the savage sense of the word." He smiled, indulgently. "The Throoby are, in fact, a uniquely placid race. Placid to the point of lethargy, one might say. Their planet is remarkably fertile, obviating any genuine necessity for cultivation. Consequently, their civilization, *per se,* is almost non-existent. Their culture, correspondingly, is also dormant."

"No music?" said Klein. He tutted.

"They have not even reached the infantile stage," said Wainwright unkindly, "of beating rhythmically on a hollow log." He favoured Klein with an acid smile.

"Cubes," said Klein, unruffled. He removed his gum from his mouth and parked it beside him on the hull. "I knocked holes in all the furniture before I was three years old."

Wainwright glared at him coldly.

"Very possibly. I had always assumed that an inherently destructive nature was conducive to drumming in a jazz band. No doubt by the time your period of demonstration is completed, you will find yourself with a race of log-beating dervishes on your hands."

Klein smiled equably and removed the wrapper from a fresh wafer of gum.

"The Throoby," said Wainwright pointedly ignoring him, "are vegetarians, which should in some measure alleviate any fears that you may entertain with regard to the possibility of being butchered and eaten. They are bipeds and vaguely humanoid in shape, although the excessive rotundity of their bodies, contrasting with the extreme length of their necks and the comparably minute dimensions of their craniums, may strike you as rather ludicrous."

"Fat little guys with pin-heads," said Greer. He winked at Klein. "Why the name Throoby?"

"The name," said Wainwright, well into his stride and moving strongly, "derives, as is the custom in cases of this type, from what appears to be their one sound of vocal communication. It involves a pursing of the lips, a singularly protuberant part of their facial features, and the emitting of a bubbling sound, the exact pronunciation of which has resulted in their consequent naming. Tests have shown that they possess a minor form of telepathy, comparatively undeveloped, due to their inherently slothful natures. It would appear…"

"Sound interesting," said Perkins. "This noise of theirs, I mean. Might come in handy for triple-tongueing, if they ever get that far. How does it go exactly, Major?"

Gratified by this interest, Wainwright pursed his lips to an alarming degree, sucking in a lungful of air as he did so.

He bubbled, plaintively.

Greer shrieked, Klein shook silently, while Perkins' laughter was confined to a high-pitched hoot. Sneider, with a superhuman effort, managed to regain control of his features.

"Great," he said. His voice was a trifle husky. "Swell. You'll have to excuse the boys, Major." Wainwright's face a dull magenta. "They have a kind of off-beat sense of humour, you might say. Never know what's going to tickle them next. There was a cross-eyed 'copter pilot one time. Kept them going for the best part of three hundred miles…" He broke off, eyeing Wainwright's purpling features with mild concern.

"Your apologies on behalf of your colleagues," said Wainwright, steaming almost visibly, "hardly exempt you from inclusion in their ranks. It was, I am sure, merely your awareness of your position of responsibility as their leader, and the consequent recipient of any unfavourable disciplinary action that may be deemed necessary, that restrained you from joining them in this infantile demonstration of misplaced humour."

Sneider scowled. "Now see here, Major…"

"*You* see here." Wainwright's expression was that of a man who fully believed himself justified by circumstances. "This expedition demands the utmost caution and tact in its mode of approach. These people are still a virtually unknown quantity as far as we are concerned. The Government has found that the majority of the less fortunate races respond extremely favourably to overtures that are accompanied by an obvious desire to share with them the benefits of our culture and technology. When offered humbly, naturally. Any trace of arrogance or idiotic demonstrations of thoughtless hilarity, such as this recent endeavour, have invariably led to unnecessarily complicated diplomatic approaches, resulting in a cripplingly high expenditure of both finances and personnel." He glowered at Sneider, who shifted uncomfortably.

"Miner VI, the domicile of the Throoby, is exceptionally rich in natural mineral deposits which will be of extreme value to our own civilization. Following the present policy of diplomatic finesse, essential in maintaining our peaceful relations with inhabited planets, the Government has tactfully refrained from imposing on the Throoby in any way, until such time as our contact with them has been made more concrete. Your mission here is not merely to entertain. You must consider yourselves diplomatic representatives of our planet, bringers of good-will, extending the hand of friendship through the medium of musical expression." His last two sentences contained a little more of his former caustic aloofness.

"You must erase the attitude nurtured by your former environment and remember that you are not engaged in presenting a jazz jamboree for the benefit of the dance-hall fraternity. A great deal may depend on your endeavours and your mental approach to them."

The ship shuddered slightly.

"We appear to be decelerating." Wainwright smoothed the front of his uniform and favoured them with a final frosty look. "I strongly advocate that you bear my remarks in mind. The future of your contract with the Culture Council will doubtless be influenced by the results that you produce here. Success will possibly mean the doubling of your present salaries. I hardly need say what might happen should your attempts prove inadequate for our purposes. If self-discipline is practised," said Wainwright kindly, "I see no reason why the Throoby should not derive a certain amount of childish pleasure from the little that you have to offer."

* * * *

The Throoby were everything that had been promised. Bubbling enthusiastically, they swarmed around the ship as the covered instruments were lowered onto the grassy plain, nodding their tiny heads approvingly on the top of their pliably hose-like necks. Their bodies were blue, toning tastefully through a mild shade of purple to crimson pink where it reached their heads.

"Good enough to eat," said Klein in an undertone, as he and Greer manoeuvred the bass through the hatch. He licked his lips in an exaggerated fashion. "They look like all-day suckers with legs."

"I thought *they* were supposed to be the savages," said Greer. He smiled in friendly fashion at Wainwright, who stood a little distance away, supervising the unloading, surrounded by a group of natives. "Better not let Pickle-puss hear you talk that way, joke or no joke. We're the Good-Behaviour Boys while he's around, else we're out on our butts. Speaking for myself, the idea of spending the rest of my days ladling out syrup in fifth-rate circuit halls has a limited appeal. This is a piece of soft soap, and we want to make it stick." He bared his teeth, genially, at a trio of the more inquisitive Throoby who insisted on trying to help and only succeeded in getting under his feet. "Smile for the pretty people, Tubs. Show 'em what a big, fat, friendly slob you can be."

The unloading was completed without mishap. Wainwright bustled over from a conference with the pilot to where a quartet of rather strained toothpaste smiles were being directed at the surrounding natives.

"For Heaven's sake," said Wainwright testily. "There's no need to overdo it. These people are perfectly well aware that our present intentions are completely friendly. You don't see me with a grin permanently plastered all over my features, do you?"

"No," said Perkins solemnly.

"Very well, then." Wainwright unzipped his brief case and fumbled inside. "The pilot tells me that I have an hour before take-off to rejoin the *Nova Queen*. My appointment with the C.C. representative on Miner VII concerns an urgent matter which will take approximately four days to conclude. We should be returning for you on Tuesday, leaving you six full days in which to attempt to awaken the population to the rewards that may be found in the production of your primitive musical sounds." He pointed to the prefabricated hut that stood a short distance away.

"You will make your quarters over there. You will find ample room for both yourselves and your equipment, and adequate supplies. There is a considerable reduction in temperature shortly after dark, but the wall insulation and battery-powered heating unit which is built into the building should maintain conditions at a reasonably comfortable level. Well." He riffled impatiently through the sheaf of papers in his hand. "We'd better make a start. If you could commence what unpacking and assembling is necessary for an initial demonstration, I shall communicate with them and inform them of the purpose of our visit. A short introductory address might prove advisable."

He adjusted the dials on the top of the espadaptor slung around his neck and wedged the earphones in position.

He turned and faced the fidgeting natives, raising his hand in formal greeting. A chorus of eager throobying greeted the gesture.

The next part of the proceedings was reminiscent of a silent movie. At intervals, Wainwright gestured expressively towards the quartet who endeavoured to entertain within the limitations of their roles, with the dramatic removal of covers from the various pieces of equipment. As each item was revealed, a fresh outburst came from the crowd. Klein got the biggest hand, a positive flood of bubbling greeting the exposure of his cymbals and trap-tray, the latter, with its luminously painted temple-blocks, receiving perhaps the noisiest reception of all.

"Well," said Wainwright, after ten minutes of silent communication. He removed the earphones and turned his back on the crowd, permitting himself the vestige of a smile. "Our intentions, at least, appear to be favourably received. Let us hope that we can maintain this interest with the ensuing cacophony. I have followed routine procedure by giving a brief history of each instrument, its origin, construction, and role in the musical world." He clicked his tongue regretfully. "The purpose of its present employment rendered the latter rather difficult at times from a musical standpoint, but I think that a sufficiently simple explanation has been offered."

He raised his eyebrows at Sneider.

"It may seem rather pointless, but I think I should announce your opening—ah—number. An announcement of some kind should precede the actual barrage, I think?"

Sneider, brow puckered, made last minute adjustments to the reed of his clarinet. Greer thrummed a run on his alloy-bodied bass. Klein replied with a brief paradiddle on the snare-drum, terminating with a softly-struck cymbal hiss. Perkins fingered the valves of his trumpet nervously.

"'Big Noise'?" said Sneider. He cleared his throat nervously. "Should give 'em some kind of idea. Spike and me'll riff two choruses in the middle. You guys split two to kick off with, then we'll follow. O.K?"

Klein nodded. Greer plucked an approving note.

Sneider turned to Wainwright. "'The Big Noise from Winnetka'."

"More aptly titled," said Wainwright, "than the bulk of your repertoire, I should imagine." He smiled thinly, adjusted the headphones and made brief communication with the goggling crowd.

He nodded at Sneider.

"One, two…"

The boom, rattle and swish that constituted the major ingredients of the nearly three-hundred-year-old classic, echoed across the surrounding landscape. Greer plucked, swayed, slapped and spun his instrument. Klein filled in, indulging in plenty of wristy stick-twirling at the same time. Greer whistled his way through the traditional eight bars. A brace of riff choruses rasped above the pounding, then bass and drums worked their way through to a fade-out finish.

The shrill bubbling was deafening. Several members of the crowd leaped up and down, their heads wobbling dangerously on their stalk-like necks. Feet stamped, enthusiastically. The quartet exchanged jubilant grins.

"They appear," said Wainwright, gratification temporarily overcoming his ingrained aversion to the music, "to approve. Very interesting and most promising. Perhaps it would be advisable to refrain from an encore until their enthusiasm has abated a little. To over-excite them may result in damage to the equipment and ourselves."

He adjusted the headphones once more, checked the dial positions and communicated with the still uproarious crowd.

It took him some little time to regain calm, but eventually the bubbling abated. Wainwright thanked them for their obviously approving reception, adding that it was gratifying to find that the efforts of his cultural ambassadors, as he referred to them, seemed able to provide their friends with a source of enjoyment that would be a further strengthening of the already strong social bond between their two races. The Throoby bubbled approvingly and a little impatiently.

"Most gratifying," said Wainwright removing the headphones once more. "There seems to be little doubt that this experiment will prove to be a boon to both sides. A much-needed stimulus, culturally on one hand, and a fresh source of essential raw material on the other. Perhaps we had better continue with the entertainment while their enthusiasm remains at its present pitch. What do you suggest as a suitable item to maintain this atmosphere of mutual goodwill?"

Sneider told him. Wainwright announced it, and graciously stepped to one side to allow the audience an unrestricted view of the quartet in action.

They swung into "Spaceport Stomp," moving nicely. Perkins provided a tight, brassy lead, with Sneider shrilling harsh-toned obligato behind him. Bass and drums thudded, steadily and unobtrusively. They were just moving into the second chorus when audience reaction set in.

The Throoby throobyed again, but this time it contained a different note. Perkins faltered, blew a few more bars, then took his trumpet from his lips, looking worried. The clarinet squeaked, solo, for a few brief moments, then tailed fumblingly into silence. Klein and Greer followed suit, looking apprehensively at Wainwright.

"What on Earth...?" said Wainwright. He looked both puzzled and upset. He fumbled feverishly with the headphones. "A sudden and definite change in reaction, undoubtedly... One almost has the feeling that they disapprove. I must clarify this immediately before we proceed any further."

He nervously patted the headphones in place, and communicated with the crowd. His expression was one of intense concentration. Several times he nodded.

When at last he removed the headphones, his face expressed relief tinged with slightly sour apology.

"It would appear," he said, "that your initial offering met with such approval that they require an encore. To be more precise, several encores. Perhaps a variation on the same theme would suffice, containing, of course, similar gymnastics on the parts of Mr. Klein and Mr. Greer. The Throoby have expressed a definite preference for the type of material that involves apparent physical exertion on the part of the performers." He addressed Sneider. "The parts played by yourself and Mr. Perkins would appear to be superfluous to their enjoyment. Perhaps it would be as well if you were to confine yourselves to an occasional brief solo passage, and nothing more, provided, that is, that the antics of your two percussionists were sufficiently distracting to maintain the interest of the audience. Possibly in time they will become accustomed to your interruptions, but at present I feel that it would merely incite them to further demonstrations of disapproval."

He lowered his eyebrows, glancing keenly at the two musicians concerned. Perkins shuffled, uncomfortably. Sneider looked pained.

"Unfortunate," said Wainwright, "but apparently necessary if we wish to remain welcome here. That, when all else is considered, is the one reason for our presence. I sincerely hope that a more favourable set of circumstances will prevail when I return in a few days. However, until such time as seems suitable for the enlargement of your roles, I must insist that you comply rigidly with the demands of your audience. Should there be no change in the situation at the termination of your visit, naturally I must turn in my assessment of the advisability of retaining wind instrumentalists in groups of a similar experimental nature."

"But I'm the lea…" said Sneider feebly.

"I fully appreciate the embarrassment that you must be feeling at finding yourself a superfluous member of your own organisation." Wainwright fixed his gaze stiffly in Sneider's direction. "You must, however, be made aware of the irrelevancy of such a situation when the picture is viewed dispassionately. The sole aim of the Council is to foster amicable relations that will result in suitably congenial conditions for trading with these people. The resulting dilemmas of one or two people can hardly bear claim to personal consideration when odds of such magnitude are at stake." He paused to clear his throat. Behind him, the Throoby expressed their dissatisfaction at the long interval by intermittent plaintive bubbling.

"Our hosts would appear to be impatient at the length of this discussion," said Wainwright. He was obviously relieved at finding an excuse to terminate the conversation. "I suggest that you continue as planned, with your colleague and yourself refraining from any interruptions that may in any way be interpreted as an attempt to be recognised as an integral part of the proceedings."

He glanced hurriedly at his watch, ignoring the brace of sullen glares directed at him. "I have approximately twenty minutes before leaving to rejoin the ship. Perhaps my time would be best employed in checking the supplies and equipment in your quarters. If you adhere to the mode of performance that I have specified, I doubt that my absence will in any way disrupt the gathering. Please proceed."

He departed hurriedly.

The thrum, thud, crash and occasional clank of a percussion duet reverberated, a trifle dully, across the alien landscape.

\* \* \* \*

"If I have to whistle one more unholy chorus," said Greer grittily, "of that unholy 'Big Noise,' I'm going to take my dog-house and wreak unholy havoc on those technicoloured jelly-bags."

It was three days later.

During the time that had elapsed since Wainwright's departure, a daily routine had been set up. In the mornings, when the insistent bubbling outside the hut became too much to bear they grumblingly assembled their gear and put in an appearance. Under normal circumstances, the reaction invoked would have been gratifying, but nullifying repetition had bleached all pleasure from the proceedings. They managed to terminate the first performance after a couple of hours, exhausting for Klein and Greer, and frustratingly boring for Sneider and Perkins, after which they straggled limply back to the hut to doze, shave, play cards, read and indulge in irritable and spasmodic conversation. Afternoons and evenings followed the same pattern.

The social atmosphere had deteriorated considerably.

The shaky positions of Sneider and Perkins had at first been discussed with a great deal of co-operative blasphemy, all of it aimed at the fortunately absent Wainwright, whose ears would have been rapidly reduced to ashes had he been present. Eventually, it was more reasonably directed at the Throoby.

Following Wainwright's departure, various experiments had been tried. Chase-choruses, frantic soloing above raucous tom-tom pounding, frenzied squealing in the vicinity of G above high C from Perkins, and similar gallery-fetching antics were all soon drowned in riotous choruses of bubbling disapproval. At the end of the second day, trumpet and clarinet were grimly packed away in their respective cases, where they remained. That morning, the thunder of drums and bass alone had assailed the surrounding countryside. The morning performance had finished a half-hour previously. Perkins was sulkily attempting to read, Klein was outside touching up his by now well-worn temple-blocks with fluorescent paint, while Sneider and Greer were seated at the table, moodily sorting through their respective rummy hands.

"You've got no cause to gripe," said Sneider. He studied the faces of seven cards that presented him with an inconceivably slender chance of laying them on the table first, and sneered. "If those technicoloured jelly-bags of yours stay tone-deaf, you're on a nonstop gravy train. *If* you choose to bust up the group, that is. After all the work…"

"What am I supposed to do?" said Greer. His sneer matched Sneider's own. "Stick with you and go back in the peanuts' parade? That's all I'd ever make if I was dumb enough to let you soft-talk me out of this. You heard what the guy said. Double pay if we could make this stick. Is it my fault you play such bum clarinet that a bunch of bubblers don't go for it? Work, he says." He appealed to Klein, who had just ambled in through the open doorway. "This guy don't know the meaning of the word 'til he's pulled his way through nine hundred and ninety-nine choruses of the 'Big Slam from Poughkeepsie'." He glowered at Sneider. "Sure, it's graft, but there's living money to be made out of it. You blame me if…?"

"Stow it," said Klein. "Knock it off. You don't have to push it in and break it." He scowled at Greer, then looked apologetically at Sneider. "You see how it is, Chick. No guy wants to beat his head to a pulp on the circuit for the rest of his life. There's no kicks in it when you get to my age. The dough Sammy and I stand to make should get us out of this in three, four years. I like working with you, fella, but what would you do in my shoes? One break like this in a lifetime…"

"O.K.," said Sneider. He was huffily morose. "You don't have to make a big spiel out of it. You got your chance, you take it. Just don't haunt me after you try your stuff out on a bunch of king-size jellyfish that don't go for tub-beating." He curled his lip at Greer. *"And* off-key gut-thumping. You guys ain't what I'd call indispensable. I've worked with classier backings from scratch outfits at church socials befo…"

*"Hey!"* bellowed Klein.

Cursing volubly, he shot outside the hut. Startled, the others joined him. He was rooting feverishly amongst his scattered equipment.

Sneider said: "What the heck…?"

"Took my paint," said Klein. He swore again, luridly, stood and waved his fist at a trio of rapidly departing natives who were headed towards the Throoby village. "They been hanging around for a half hour, gawping at it, the lousy pink and blue crooks. Special stuff, it was. Three credits a can and hard to get. When I get my hands…"

Sneider laughed sharply.

"Three credits! This is the guy that's all set for easy-street in three, four years. One thing I never could figure was a tight-wad. The more they got," he confided in Perkins, "the more they want."

"Tight-wad?" said Klein. He was breathing heavily. He thrust out his jaw. "Seems to me I recall a poker game on the trip here when a full-house…"

"For the love of Pete," said Perkins wearily. "Don't you guys every let go one another's throats? This is like open-house at a back-biters' convention. I'm taking a walk." He went a few paces, turned. "You coming, chief?"

"Right with you," said Sneider. He glowered at Klein, went inside the hut and shrugged into his jacket. He exchanged a final nasty look with Greer on his way out. "Don't go away, Big Noise. Somebody might run off with your four-stringed gold mine."

There was a short silence after they left. Klein and Greer hauled the drums inside. Greer stacked the cards, absently, spat, and glanced at Klein.

"Want to lose your shirt, fat man? You can afford it, now your ship's come in."

Klein snorted, shook his head, and eased a finger round the inside of his collar.

"Kind of stuffy in here," he said. He pulled his mouth down at the corners and looked grim. "Should be a couple of hours before they start howling for the matinee. Why don't we leg it out of here for a while? This place locks up pretty tight."

"Suits me," said Greer. He grinned sourly. "Serve those, soreheads right if they have to cool their heels on the mat for a while. I only hope they get back before we do."

He stuffed a packet of cigarettes in his pocket, rose and kicked his chair under the table.

"O.K., Columbus. Let's go exploring."

* * * *

The day was mild, providing pleasant conditions for walking. An hour and a half later Klein and Greer, feeling the strain of unaccustomed exercise, topped the rise that brought them within sight of the hut. They stopped abruptly.

Smoke was pouring from the building, thick, grey clouds billowing through the ventilation grilles and beneath the door. As they stood, their jaws hanging slackly, a pale flicker of flame showed briefly through a window.

"The gear," said Klein hoarsely. "How the...?"

They activated themselves, desperately and raced down the short incline and across the grassy, bush-dotted plain. Greer swore pantingly as he ran. Klein pushed his bulk along wheezily, lagging a short way behind. They were halfway there when Sneider and Perkins appeared in the distance on the far side of the hut. They stopped briefly, shouted something, then charged in from their side. Greer was the first to arrive. A cloud of sparks shot out at him as the door collapsed from his kick. Smoke billowed, thickly. Klein wheezed onto the scene, Sneider and Perkins seconds later. Greer whirled, his face working furiously.

"Which of you...?"

"Don't be a chump," snarled Sneider. He gritted his teeth, his chest heaving. "You think we'd be dumb enough to start a thing like this? If we..."

"Dumb enough!" spat Greer. "Or mad enough! I'm not forgetting the way things are! Lousy spite would be enough to give a cloth head like you an idea like..."

"Can it!" said Klein, wheezily. He ran a dry tongue over his lips, panting hard. "While you two stand around insulting each other, what there is left goes up in smoke! Why don't somebody go in there and haul out what ain't burning?"

A tongue of flame licked nastily through the open doorway. Sneider bowed and indicated the opening.

"After you, pot-roast. That's all you'll be if you try playing fireman. We'd frazzle in there." He snorted, disgustedly, turned his back on the fire and slumped on the ground. "Let it burn itself out. There ain't a thing we can do about it." He glanced viciously at Greer. "Maybe I'm out of a job, but I'm still breathing. My stick's insured. So am I, but I don't collect a cent if I ain't around to put in a claim."

Greer opened his mouth, growled and shut it again. He spat, lumbered a short distance and sank to the ground. Klein joined him silently. Perkins deposited himself beside Sneider.

Morosely, four pairs of eyes gloomed at the horizon.

The fire, exhausting the supply of inflammable material, soon died. The shell of the hut was fireproof and still intact, but unbearably hot when they tried to enter. They let it cool for half an hour, and then ventured inside.

Klein's cymbals, stands and the metal shells of his drums were intact, but the skins were gone, also his sticks. Only the clips of his temple-blocks remained on the trap-tray. The body of Greer's bass was unharmed, but the strings were gone. A jumble of blackened keys and the hinges and spring-clip of his case, almost buried in a pile of ash, were all that remained of Sneider's clarinet. Parkins' trumpet alone remained a possibly playable instrument, but the lacquer was peeling away and it was covered in grime. All clothing, bedding and supplies were reduced to ashes.

"Great," said Perkins angrily. He gingerly touched his trumpet, removed his hand hastily and sucked his fingers. "This makes me a hot trumpet player all right. When this thing cools off, I'll give our friends a solo and blow soot all over them."

"Here's the joker that started it," said Klein. He was bent over the remains of the heating unit. "It was like an oven in here when we left. Must have kept on loading till something started it sparking. It don't happen often, but there's always the outside chance…"

"It didn't occur to you, I suppose," said Sneider bitterly, "to switch it off? If you knew what was happening, why the heck didn't you…?"

"Quiet," said Perkins. He flapped a hand. "Listen."

A bubbling mutter was growing louder outside. Greer went to the door, peered out and turned a grimly-smiling face back to the others.

"Our audience," he said. "For the afternoon clambake." He glanced at the charred remains of the espadaptor that Wainwright had left behind. "How do we tell them the good news? The magic box looks as though it might be out of commission. If we just don't show they'll be in here to drag us out. I don't know if they know what a neck-tie party is, but there's a bunch of trees about half a mile away that might have been made to order. If we give them long enough to think about it, they might consider experimenting. I don't fancy ending up," said Greer biting his lip thoughtfully, "looking like one of the locals."

"Why don't we just take the stuff outside?" said Perkins. "Show them what's left. They can't be so dumb they won't be able to figure out what's happened. When they realise maybe they'll let us alone until Wainwright gets back. If we look sad enough about it…"

"Good enough," said Sneider. He was still depressed, but Perkins' remarks made sense. "Here." He grabbed a couple of cymbal stands. "Let's move this stuff out, fast."

Everything was still hot, but just bearable from the carrying point of view. They trooped outside, dumped the remains in a heap on the grass and studied the audience apprehensively.

Obviously word had got around to the neighbouring tribes. The crowd was the largest yet. Something in the region of five hundred faces beamed expectantly in their direction. Anticipatory bubbling came from the ranks of the newcomers. There was an excited swaying of necks and shuffling of feet.

"Of all the luck," said Sneider bitterly. He creased his brow at the crowd and groaned. "They had to let the neighbours in on it." He took a deep breath and stepped forward. "Wish me luck. If anything breaks it's every man for himself."

He raised a hand. The bubbling died.

He picked up the shell of the snare-drum and gestured at it. He pushed his fist through to demonstrate.

"Skin," he said loudly. "Gone. Burned. Kaput. Blooey. Noise-maker, gone." He dropped it and pointed at the bass drum. He put his foot through the gaping aperture. "Big noise. Boom, boom. No more. Poof." He waved his arms, flapped a hand at the smoke-blackened hut. "Fire…hey, that's it!" He groped for his cigarette lighter, found it, and delved into his other pockets. "Any of you guys got a piece of paper?"

Greer found his packet of cigarettes, tore the wrapper from it and handed it over. Sneider clicked the switch of the lighter and held the glowing end to the paper. It flared up He knelt quickly by the shell of the bass drum and held it in the aperture. "Fire. Burned. Got it?" He looked hopefully at the crowd.

The woebegone expressions of the Throoby made it clear that something had got through. The quartet exchanged glances of relief. Perkins blew out his breath sharply.

"Nice going, chief. At least they know what happened. The only snag is they don't know *why* it happened. I only hope you don't have to try and mime a heating unit overloading. Might be entertaining, but kind of…oh, oh. What's the big conference about?"

He looked apprehensively at the gathering.

The Throoby were gathered in a great circle, the backs of the nearest towards them. Heads nodded, and faint bubblings were heard.

Sneider backed and stood with the others. He licked his lips nervously. "What goes on?"

The Throoby solemnly exchanged views on the distressing turn of events. Plaintive enquiries were made as to why the Short-Necks had done this inexplicable thing. Thoughts wrangled freely until an elder made himself heard above the cross-current of wild conjectures.

The reason, the elder suggested kindly, should be obvious, even to the meanest intelligence among those present. Various suggestions had been made that ranged from the remotely possible to the ridiculous. A form of sacrifice was the answer. Had they not just witnessed a demonstration that symbolised the purging by fire, strongly reminiscent of their own Epocian Rites? The old was to be replaced with the new. And surely his people were not foolish enough to believe that the Beautiful Sounds were destroyed? The Instruments were merely the means of transmitting the Sounds from the Short-Necks themselves. If memory served him correctly, the Short-Neck-Who-Came-And-Went had made reference to the origin of the vanished parts, in his address preceding the first entertainment. For the benefit of those present whose memories were less efficient than his own, he explained these points again.

His companions bubbled excitedly. Several of them paid tribute to his diligence and acute sense of reasoning. Of course! The Short-Neck-Who-Came-And-Went had pointed the way to rectification of the catastrophe. True, it did seem a little drastic, but doubtless the four Short-Necks in their midst accepted such a contingency as the ultimate peak of their usefulness.

The Throoby turned.

The quartet retreated.

The crowd thinned to a circle that surrounded them and moved in, bubbling soothingly…

* * * *

The scout ship returned late on the afternoon of the sixth day. The pilot was the first outside. He studied the scene, frowning, and called through the lock to Wainwright, who was having a little trouble with his seat harness.

"Better get out here quick, Major. There's been an accident. Fire by the look of it."

Wainwright hastily freed himself, and joined the pilot on the scorched grass outside. He gaped at the hut, his normal aplomb shattered, his face pale.

"What in Heaven's…?"

He hurried to the blackened building, inspected the contents and came outside again. He looked puzzled.

"Unless they were removed afterwards, it would appear that they were absent at the time of the conflagration." He tugged at his chin nervously. "In which event they must be somewhere in the immediate vicinity. Possibly the natives ..."

He cocked his head suddenly.

In the distance, from the direction of a clump of trees, a dull thumping could be heard.

"Ahhhhhh!" Wainwright expelled a sigh of relief. He mopped his brow and the back of his neck with his handkerchief. "Following the destruction of their accommodation and supplies, they appear to have had the good sense to establish themselves in the nearest spot offering reasonable shelter from the night elements."

He replaced his handkerchief in his sleeve, straightened his jacket and commenced walking briskly in the direction of the sounds.

"In a purely musical sense, the situation would appear to have undergone little change since my departure. The only alteration being, possibly, a further deterioration in the standard of musicianship." As they neared the trees Wainwright winced. "An *appalling* cacophony!"

"I've heard better drumming than that," said the pilot dryly, "from a one-armed two-year-old."

They entered the trees and came to a clearing. They halted abruptly.

Light filtered faintly through the thickly-meshed foliage overhead. An audience of natives was seated, their backs towards the visitors, bubbling contentedly, their gaze directed towards the centre of the clearing.

A Throoby was seated on a log, behind a battery of equipment that Wainwright recognised.

The overall condition of the drums appeared to have deteriorated in some way, but several items seemed spotlessly clean. The four temple-blocks, which appeared, vaguely, to his inexperienced eye, larger than before, glowed with a dim orange fluorescence. The various tautly-stretched drum-heads, too, seemed in immaculate condition. These, the Throoby was enthusiastically beating with a brace of slim white objects that appeared oddly to have a knob at either end.

They were moving too fast in the dimness to be positively identified as drum sticks.

Beside him two more natives were ineffectually producing noises from Greer's metal-bodied bass. One sat precariously on the other's almost non-existent shoulders, plucking at the strings that seemed unusually slack and difficult to grasp. The other supported the instrument from below. The sounds produced were uneven in tempo and repetitive.

Wainwright stared, puzzled.

"Well," said the pilot. He strained his eyes against the gloom and shrugged. "No sign of our friends, if they *are* anywhere around." He bit his lip. "Could be they're resting up somewhere while the class enjoys itself." He peered at the drummer, and snorted. "Our fat friend had better get back here quick before something…"

He shook his head and blinked.

"Darndest thing. Could almost have sworn those blocks were grinning at us."

They were.

# WILLIE'S BLUES

*Thursday, September 17th, 1936*
*Room 24, Taylor House Hotel, Florence, South Carolina*

The drive here gave me my first real chance to see rural America, 1936 style. Incredibly restful, almost too much so. I found myself dozing at the wheel a couple of times, a highly dangerous thing to do. The car has behaved itself pretty well, but I still can't get used to actually having to steer the damn thing myself.

Florence is nothing special, what I've seen of it so far; could be any small town. The Freemont hall where they're playing tonight is right down the street from here, half a block away on the other side. They've got posters outside, confirming the date I got from the booking agency, so at least I'll be spared hanging around here any longer than I have to.

Not much traffic down there at the moment, certainly no band buses in sight, so it looks as though they're still on their way from Portland.

Come on, Willie baby.

*Friday, September 18th, 1936*
*Room 24, Taylor House Hotel, Florence, South Carolina*

It's a little after 2:00 A.M., and I've just finished rewriting history.

I still can't grasp it. I thought I was coming here to plug the gaps in our own records, but instead I've been finding out just what they mean at the transfer centre when they talk about the past, present and future being interlinked in ways that we haven't even begun to understand yet.

I feel drunk. I suppose the whisky has something to do with it, but it's more emotional than alcoholic. To find out that you're a part of something like this, a *real* part—

Good God. Can it really mean that without my intervention he would have spent the rest of his life skulking around in musical vacuums like Curry's crowd? Surely it couldn't be! A talent like that would be bound to get kicked out into the open by *something*. It just isn't—

But—what *else* could have done it?

I must get this down in detail now, before I go to bed. I might have lost some of it by morning if I don't. Hell, my head feels as if its one ambition is to float up and nestle against the ceiling. I shouldn't think my chances of getting hold of any coffee are very bright, either. This place is like the rest of the town, lights out by one o'clock at the very latest. Better try walking around. I only hope the fellow underneath is asleep by now—*and* that he sleeps heavy.

First impressions. A small man who looks like an apologetic version of his photographs, playing in a pretty indifferent band. The acoustics were abominable, but even so it was possible to tell that the records made at the time hadn't lied. The whole thing was a scrappy echo of what the Curry band of five or six years earlier had done so well, and the crowd knew it, too. This is only a medium-sized country town, but even a semi-rural bunch like that listen to the radio and know the difference. They applauded, but it was more good manners than enthusiasm.

He took no solos. All the tenor breaks were handled by Claude Perry, playing a thin pastiche of what Joe Pitman was doing with them before he went off to make it on his own. And Turnhill just sat there, blowing when the sheets told him to; a musician doing a job. I really wanted to scream. The whole thing was insane, with something uniquely unreal about it; ghosts, mimicking echoes from a glorious past, with the only real talent there confined to section work. Ludicrous. I'd been running the machine, but I didn't waste thread when it became obvious that Turnhill wasn't going to be given any space at all.

It finished just after twelve and I went outside with the rest of the crowd, fetched the car, and parked it across from the front of the hall. It was raining, something that I thought of at the time as a lucky break, but I see it a little differently now, of course. It was an ingredient, in exactly the same way that I was; a scheduled event that could no more have failed to happen than I could have prevented myself from being here right now, talking into this microphone.

Anyway, he came out on his own, the last one to leave. The rest of them had already beat it to different parts of town, towing local girls with them. He was wary when I hailed him and offered him a lift, but he didn't have a topcoat and it was raining pretty steadily by then. He got in the back, gave me directions, and off we went.

To put him at his ease, I went straight into my electronics engineer/jazz buff from Baltimore routine; how I'd been passing through town when I'd seen the posters advertising Jerome Curry and his Famous Band, and decided to stay over for the night, and so on. I went on to say that I'd heard him once or twice with Benny Case when I'd been in Michigan a couple of years before, and couldn't understand why he wasn't getting any solo space with Curry.

He said his style hadn't fitted in too well, and I didn't find that too hard to believe. Curry had been good about it, though, he said, keeping him on the while he worked on his tone. He'd bought a new mouthpiece to help him thicken it up a little, the way they'd specified he should.

I felt an uncomfortable prickling around the scalp at that point, the first hint that things weren't as I'd expected them to be. The statement itself was bad enough, of course, but what really worried me was the off-hand way that it was delivered. Here was the man who was going to have more influence on the distilling of the music than anybody else in its entire history, placidly telling me that he was in the process of mutilating the most sublime instrumental tone I ever heard, and talking about it in the same way that he might have discussed wearing a different kind of hat.

The conversation died completely for maybe half a minute while I digested this, or tried to, and then I asked him what his plans were, whether he intended sticking with Curry or perhaps trying his luck in surroundings that might offer him a little more scope.

I'd expected at least a glimmer of discontent in his answer, some small hint of restiveness, but again, nothing, and this time my hair really rose. He made some vague remark about New York, a new cooperative band, but it was obviously a straight lie, prompted by what was left of his vanity.

He didn't really want to try his luck in New York, or anywhere else. It was impossible to imagine a more ludicrous candidate for revolution, but there he was; a man who honestly seemed to think that he'd found his slot and was staying in it as long as he could, thickening up his tone the way they'd told him to and glad of the chance to commit such a crime.

We reached where he was staying, and I stopped the car, wondering what the hell was going on. Although I still had no inkling that I was in any way essential to the pattern of events, I did have the feeling at that point that to let him go without trying to work on him in some way, soften him up a little, would be a mistake. So, on the spur of the moment, as he was getting out of the car, I asked him if he'd like to come on over here for a drink.

He didn't dither too much this time. I'd more or less established my credentials by then, and the place he was booked into was a drab, unwelcoming hole. He said thanks, sat down again, and we headed back into town.

His relief at my invitation had been pretty obvious, and I began to get a bit more of the picture.

He was twenty-six years old, a professional musician for ten of these, but despite that he was still a small-town boy from Oklahoma, still painfully shy, and the fact that his head had gradually filled with ideas and sounds like nobody else's had proved to be no asset in his present employment.

It must have been an almost traumatic experience in some ways, after painfully building himself a minor reputation in territory bands; the chance of playing with a name band on the skids when Curry found himself stuck for a tenor in mid-tour, the reactions of the older, relatively established musicians, gradually corroding what little confidence he'd ever had, until finally this; a small, confused, tired man, gratefully snapping up the stale crumbs that they threw his way.

It was murder, pure and simple. But somewhere along the way I knew that he was going to hear the Sam Lacey band, and that was to be the turning point. I sweated with relief when I remembered that, knowing it for a solid fact that had been entered in the history books a long, long time before I was even born, something that, no matter what was said and done prior to the event, had actually happened.

Feeling better, I asked him if he'd heard the Lacey band, and he said he hadn't. He'd met Lacey, though, had gigged with him a few times around Scranton, but he didn't know anything about him getting his own group together.

It was right then when it hit me, and I still don't really know why. It was as though I'd turned a page in an until then incomprehensible story and suddenly found myself looking at the key to the whole thing, the piece of the puzzle around which everything else fitted and without which none of what was happening right then would have made any sense at all; my actual trip back to this time, the two days in Kansas City when I'd visited the Blackjack Club, our meeting that evening, my choice of "profession"; all of them slipping smoothly into place and making beautiful sense, without a seam showing anywhere.

What had happened up until then had shaken me, but this was something else again. It frightened me then and it frightens me now, because it's confirmed a suspicion that I've had all my life and which I've deliberately avoided thinking about too much, for the simple reason that I didn't want to run the risk of convincing myself that it really was so.

But it's happened, and there's no going back. In short, what it means is that free will is just an expression, a myth founded on vanity and wishful thinking; that every single mote in the universe is committed to exist in time and space only according to the specification. The interaction of time that they talked about at the transfer centre is even more of an involved fact than they perhaps dream, and my mind is still blundering along after the concept, unable to get more than an occasional and all too brief grip on it.

Dear Jesus—every step that I take around this room, every movement that I've ever made, every syllable that I'm saying right now; all of it indelibly printed on the circuit, each inflection a response that it's impossible to break or even bend, just a little.

Where did I get to? Fetched him back here, right. I sat him down and poured drinks and gradually got him to open up about himself, prompting him every time he started to slow down and crawl back into his shell.

It's on thread, and it'll make an interesting exercise in sifting fact from fiction when I get around to working on it. He was a pretty pathetic character in a lot of ways at that point, but I can't honestly say that I spent a lot of time feeling sorry for him.

After all, how do you feel pity for a god that you know is standing on the threshold of his kingdom? If he'd been given the choice, I don't think he would have hesitated for a minute in choosing the way that he was destined to go, and I doubt that there are many people who would really want to trade long-lived anonymity for that kind of glory, however brief.

We drank and talked for about half an hour, and then I went over to my suitcase and fooled around, making it look as though I had the recorder in there instead of my jacket pocket. I dug out the thread with the Lacey band on it, changed it with the one I'd been using during the evening, and then showed it to him. I told him it was something I'd been working on for a while, an experimental model, but I hadn't been able to iron out a few bugs just yet so that it would be marketable.

I stuck it between us on the carpet, switched on, and then sat back, confidently waiting for the big awakening.

It didn't take long for it to dawn on me that his reactions were hardly those of a man who was at long last seeing the light at the end of the tunnel. I hadn't expected him to leap to his feet shouting "Eureka!" or anything like that, but all I was getting was guarded approval, completely in character with what had gone before.

He drank and tapped his foot, and every so often he would smile a little and say that this or that was O.K. He did criticize the tenor player—he said he thought he was a little busy for that kind of outfit—but even this came out of a kind of apology, as though he thought I might bounce back at him for having the nerve to put down somebody that I personally might think was pretty good.

Again, I couldn't believe it. I sat there, staring at him, my piece of history shrivelling like a deceptively bulging paper bag that had been holding nothing but air after all. The situation had degenerated into pure nightmare this time. There might have been the faintest shadow of wistfulness somewhere in his eyes, but it didn't disturb the other things that I saw there. He was still small, still frightened; too smart to take any real notice of siren songs like the one he was hearing then, too battered by experience to consider venturing from his small corner to add his own voice to it.

After a while, there was a knock on the door. It was the manager, asking me to cut the noise down in response to a complaint from the room underneath. I apologized, and when he'd gone I switched off the machine and sat down again feeling like the biggest damn fool in all creation.

It seemed to be a total impasse. I thought that I'd stumbled across the real facts as opposed to the inevitable distortions of historic records, but now it looked as though I'd simply jumped to the wrong conclusions, probably steered there by some childishly vain part of my subconscious.

But the records had been wrong, anyway. He'd heard Lacey now, and if he were all fired up to race off to Kansas City, he certainly had me fooled. It's always been common belief, supposedly backed by his own testimony, that he'd heard the band on the radio and straightaway wired them, offering Lacey his services. But the moment of encounter had come and gone, and he was still the same vaguely shifty nonentity that he'd been before; liking what he'd heard, that had been obvious enough, but showing not the slightest sign that he'd been stirred sufficiently to even consider leaving Curry of his own volition.

He hadn't been fired, that was pretty certain. There's an interview that Curry gave to *Downbeat* magazine in the nine-teen-forties, where he confirmed that Turnhill had walked out on the band during a tour, this tour. So *something* had yanked him up out of his rut and set him running, but whatever it was it wasn't Lacey's music.

There was another ingredient that hadn't shown itself yet, lurking somewhere just along the way; something so potent that it had reached right down through the fear and shattered confidence and ignited what was buried somewhere there underneath it all.

And then I got it, my second and conclusive flash of realization, and my immediate reaction was "My God, I can't possibly do it."

The reason for this was simple enough. I've broken a cardinal rule laid down by the transfer people, and at that moment the fear of possible resulting restrictions being placed on the rest of my programme if it was found out was all that concerned me. But gradually I began to get it in proportion, because it was obvious that this was going to be the only possible way to stir him from the awful apathy that was pinning him down.

And again, I saw that this was further evidence that the transfer people still don't really appreciate what they're tampering with. The rule itself is clear and on the face of it perfectly reasonable and logical, but only because the workings of time still aren't understood and probably never will be completely. When they say that apart from essential equipment absolutely nothing originating further along the time-line must be taken back, their reasoning is just plain wrong. The rule is pointless, because any such action and its results have already happened.

The pattern is set, and if some lunatic, in a misguided attempt to benefit humanity long before it's due, is going to bring back the formula for curing cancer a hundred years before it's found, then it's simply not going to work. It couldn't. Something would be bound to stop it, even if the ingredients for periducium were available now, which I guess they are; lab equipment that hasn't been invented yet, or maybe something even more obvious. But whatever it was, the line would break down somehow, because everything has its place in the sequence, and there it stays.

I'm starting to ramble again. Walk and concentrate, that's all I must do right now.

My cancer cure was on thread, tucked away at the bottom of my suitcase, but this one was on schedule, I knew it. My reasons for compiling it and bringing it along had been simple enough, or so I'd thought at the time. By putting the absolute cream on one spool, the very best of the music that had ever been issued commercially, I felt that I was taking along the equivalent of a favourite book, one that you can pick up and re-read any time you feel the need for something familiar in an alien place.

But now I knew the real reason, and I almost laughed out loud at the sheer contrary poetry of it.

The visit of the hotel manager had shaken him quite a bit. There'd been no one at the desk when we'd come in; so I'd helped myself to my key, and although I'd instinctively had the sense to hold the conversation in the doorway so that he hadn't been seen, the simple fact of his being there at all, a Negro in a white man's hotel room late at night, the setting for a disturbance even as minor as the one we'd made, had stirred him to a kind of fear that only people of his time and circumstance could really understand.

Thanks to my prolonged silence, he was on his feet and muttering that he had to go by the time I'd more or less sorted out my own confusion. I poured him another drink and said there was just one more thing I wanted him to hear, get his opinion on. I kept the conversation going while I dug out the spool, saying that I'd picked it up on a K.C. waveband on a recent trip and thought it pretty fine, but didn't have any idea who it could be. Maybe he'd know.

He fidgeted and sneaked glances at his watch and the door, but he obviously didn't want to cause offence by beating it out of here in too much of a hurry. I reset the spool, taking the tone control right back so that the sound would be a little muddy and, I hoped more authentic, put the recorder on the dresser this time, turned the volume down a little, and switched on.

It got him, almost from the first bar; not hooking him completely, but enough to stop his dithering around, as though he'd had most of his motor reflexes switched off. It's a track that I've probably played more than any other and it's never failed to electrify me, but the circumstances then were magnifying its power to a pitch that it had never reached before. Lacey's opening solo, the simplest and probably the most effective one he ever recorded, with that filigree of single notes in the fifth and sixth bars and the final bump he gives to the chord in the tenth; in a way, it was hitting me as hard as it was hitting him.

And when the tenor came in with that sublime descending figure, laying it across the twelfth bar and then pushing into the second chorus, it was as though he'd suddenly been kicked in the solar plexus. He bent at the knees and sank back on to his chair again, leaning forward the whole time. He looked almost sick, jaw hanging, sweat showing around his nose and mouth. His feet stayed still to start with, but then they began to move; gently, barely lifting off the floor, but he could no more have kept them still than he could have flown.

It was the moment of revelation, all right; a kind of aural surgery that was showing him his own piece of genius underneath all the muck that had accumulated around it and stifled it to near-extinction.

My own feelings at this juncture were pretty mixed, and they still are. "Willie's Blues" was the finest thing he ever committed to record, but I couldn't help remembering that it had been his last recording, too, made when he must have been a pretty sick man. To be his saviour, that was fine. But what would have happened if I hadn't been? Would he have lived longer? Would he have ever got started on his notorious overindulgence in just about every single thing that it doesn't pay to overindulge in, after diving straight into the deep end of the pool that he'd been scared to even dip his toe in all those years?

He might have married, raised a family, got out of the music business altogether; found a less demanding slot for himself somewhere, a life where he might even have been happy in the low-keyed way that most people are at least a part of the time.

I'm just being maudlin about this, I guess. He could just as easily have been knocked down by a car or got himself killed in the war, anything at all, really. No, I didn't exactly do him a complete disservice, and it's on the record that he'll live the time he has left right up to the hilt, something that only happens to the handful who find themselves deified in that special way.

The music finished, and he sat there like a statue for maybe ten, fifteen seconds without speaking.

Then he asked me who it was, in a gritty kind of whisper, like someone struggling to surface from a deep trance. I said I didn't know. Static, I improbably lied, had cut in just as it had finished, and in fiddling around with the station dial I'd lost it for good.

He believed me, I suppose, because he had no real choice. He got up and began pacing around, not speaking, his face still dull with shock. I said I guessed that Kansas City was throwing up a lot of good new people just then and that it must have been a tough job keeping up with everything that was happening there and elsewhere. He said he guessed so, hut he hadn't really heard me. He was still listening to the music inside his head, struggling to accept the fact of something that even in his wildest dreams he'd never believed could really exist outside his own imagination.

He paced some more, and then he wandered to the door, saying that he had to go, that they had a long haul the next day and he'd better snatch some sleep before getting back on the road. I don't recall him saying anything while I drove him back to his rooming house, just thanks and so long when we got there, and then he went inside without looking back.

And that's about it. God, I'm beat. As far as he's concerned it's been like opening the door to another world, his personal vision of Paradise. For me, it's different, and simply knowing the finish while I went through all those incredible preliminaries hasn't made it the kind of experience that I'm in any hurry to go through again.

And how about the sixty-four billion dollar paradox? Without me, would it have happened at all? Any of it, or any of the things that developed from it? Or would he have stayed right where he was, fouling up his tone until the sounds and shapes were buried for good and all, turning him into a walking grave-yard for some of the most sublime music to grace a part of history that wasn't exactly notable for either sublimity or grace?

Go to bed, Palmer. Even if I had a clear head I wouldn't be able to dent that one, and right now I couldn't think my way through the alphabet.

Good night, Willie baby. The shadows aren't going to be around again for quite a while now, and you've got songs to sing. Sweet dreams, and I'll be seeing you.

*Saturday, February 6th, 1937*
*Room 31, Brooks Hotel, Kansas City*

It turns out that the great night was cold and misty, and I mean cold. This room has a radiator that makes a hell of a lot of noise but works well enough in its own way; so I'm getting this down while I thaw out.

It was a great night, and not just because of its historical significance. The thread I made has done it even less than justice, I'm sure, but I guess that was inevitable. The place was jammed to the doors; great atmosphere, but it meant that the music suffered, and I was only able to pick them up from one side of the room, right next to a particularly vocal bunch of customers, who'll have come over loud and clear, I imagine.

But what a band it is now! It could be argued that they're still rough—collectively, that is—but that would be finicking for its own sake. It was incredible, like the pulse of the universe. And Willie—

I'm going to be hearing him under better conditions than this, of course, but even through all that damned extraneous racket there was something special there tonight. It was the sheer poise of the man and what he could produce in a hectic setup like that which impressed me so much.

Smoke and noise all around him, people yelling in his face, and it was as if he really were off in a world of his own. He had to be, I guess, or else it just wouldn't have been possible to create that kind of subtly intricate and beautifully controlled line. I don't know whether or not he was high, or even if he's really on anything much yet, but I suppose it was likely, with Clay there and so much hinging on the way he reacted.

But how he *swings*! Across the beat, behind it, juggling it like a man with six hands and all the time in the world; the most beautiful natural of them all, now that he's found his way. It makes me sweat, just thinking about it. A touch of parental pride, no doubt.

The Blackjack hasn't changed since my first visit, despite the increase in business. It's the usual kind of trap; longish and thin, and with a crowd in there you can't really hear much of what's happening if you're at the back of the room. The band was still jammed up in the top left-hand corner, and if there'd been more than nine of them the management would have had to chop a piece out of the bar, something I don't imagine they'd have seriously considered doing.

I got as close as I could, up against the side wall about four or five yards away, and with just enough clearance to get some kind of fix on them. It was an exhausting business, though, and I've got a pretty good idea now what it must feel like to be a sardine caught up in an earthquake, if such a thing is conceivable. I didn't actually see Clay until I was leaving, but the bunch hovering around the table nearest to the band and laughing too much and too loud gave me a pretty good idea of where he was.

Most of the time, of course, I kept my eyes on Willie. It's hard to believe that this poker-faced, totally assured man is only five months older than he was at the time of our first meeting; difficult, in fact, to believe that he's the same person at all.

The telescoping of the two occasions has underlined it, of course, but even so it's an almost ludicrous transformation. He generates the kind of detached arrogance that only a few people ever really achieve; complete and utter self-confidence, the kind that's impregnable because its foundations are built on a virtually unshakable belief in what they can do.

In actual physique he's hardly altered at all, but I have the impression of someone twice the size he was. It's Lacey's band, and in a deceptively self-effacing way he has the aura of a leader about him, but the spotlight is almost exclusively reserved for Willie, and already he's pretty close to being infallible, the personification of all that's good and right in the music.

The evening ended a little differently to what I'd expected. It certainly hadn't been part of my plans to actually meet up with him again, not at this stage, but that's what happened. The session had finished, and Clay, all smiles, was button-holing Willie as I squeezed my way out; so it came as something of a surprise when I found him grabbing my arm, fifty yards or so away from the club.

He told me he'd spotted me in the crowd just before the close, and asked what I was doing in K.C. I said hello, and told him I'd been passing through on my way from Baltimore and had made a point of looking in at the Blackjack because I'd heard from a local acquaintance that he was playing there with Lacey; news, I said, that had come as something of a surprise after what he'd said at our first meeting.

It didn't rattle him one bit. He just gave me an appraising kind of look, and then he told me about Leonard Clay showing up from New York that evening and how he was back there at the club talking business with Lacey at that moment; so I'd been right there on the spot when the big break had come. I congratulated him, saying that it had obviously been a smart move whichever way you looked at it, his leaving Curry, and that in that case I'd certainly be seeing him again soon as the company I worked for had just opened a New York office, and I hoped to fix things so that I spent a fair amount of my time there.

He said that would be fine, and then he asked the question that had been his sole reason for following me outside and which had kept him standing there in a thin band-jacket in a temperature that couldn't have been too many degrees above zero, the way it felt to me.

He asked if I'd ever got a lead on the tenor player on that last thing I'd played him, the one that I said I'd picked up on a Kansas City station.

I said I hadn't, acted surprised, and asked him if he'd drawn a blank, too. He stared at me for a moment before answering, the only outward trace of uncertainty that he showed, and then he said, no, he hadn't been able to locate him, either. But what he couldn't understand, he said, was that nobody else in the region had ever heard of anyone who was playing along remotely similar lines to his own, let alone the calibre of musician that he'd described to knowledgeable locals.

Was I sure it had been a K.C. station, or could it have been coming from somewhere else?

I felt I had to let him off the hook a little at this point. I could see that the situation had reached a stage where its plausibility was rubbing a little thin, and some sort of explanation, at least a possibility, was needed to bolster it up again. He'd already given me a suitable opening, but I didn't want to appear too eager to go along with the first suggestion that was made; so I said I was pretty sure it had been local, although it had been too long ago to swear with absolute certainty.

Maybe, I suggested, it had been some kid who'd managed to get himself a little air time before he got knocked down by a truck, something like that.

He wouldn't buy that one at all. He said, no, that kind of playing was too mature for any kid to have produced, and besides, if anything like that had happened it would have been talked about.

What we'd heard, he said, had been music with a lot of years and experience behind it; adult music, that consisted of a lot more than just technical virtuosity and an individual sound. I said that in that case it must have come from somewhere else, that I must have misread the dial setting at the time, which in turn had probably been the reason why I hadn't been able to re-locate the station.

In all probability, I said, he'd be turning up in New York one of these days if he hadn't already; so they'd be almost bound to meet eventually.

He said he supposed so. He was shivering quite a lot by then; so I said I had to go, that I'd look him up in New York when I was there and maybe we could have a drink sometime. He said O.K., we shook hands, and I came back here, not too sorry that the conversation was over. Quite apart from finding myself in a situation where I'd had to come up with some convincing lies at extremely short notice, something that I'm not normally too good at, this whole business is beginning to make me uneasy, almost squeamish in a sense.

The effect of that business in Florence, when he was virtually shown his own soul—how did it really hit him? It must have been a pretty cataclysmic encounter, stirring up echoes of a very special kind; from the future instead of the past, showing him not just what might have been, but what in fact *could* be.

It's a relief to know that he's at least going to hang on to his sanity, because no crazy man could have cut "Willie's Blues". But although this whole thing is out of my hands and I'm only going through motions that have been delegated to me, I'm still having trouble with my conscience. Stupid, really.

Every time I start thinking like this I get a headache, and it isn't to be wondered at. At least it can't be as bad as the one they're suffering from at the transfer centre, ever since I turned in my report on my first trip, I must say they took it quite well, considering that it came from a layman, but it's obviously given them a lot of rethinking to do.

My headache isn't going to improve if I stick by this radiator. It sounds as though there's somebody inside the damned thing, trying to break out with a hammer. Home, James, and I hope the climate there is the same as it was when I left, 70° in the shade.

*Wednesday, May 12th, 1937*
*Room 104, Spicer's Hotel, New York*

One more for the books, and this one qualified for the battle of the century, all five solid hours of it. Just watching and listening is exhausting enough, but that's the amazing thing. They thrive on it; not exactly unaided in a lot of cases, admittedly, but the level of coherence rarely seems to suffer.

Pitman got back from France today, and it was obvious from the way he walked into the place—Cummings' Playhouse—that he was out to get Willie. The word must have got around, because the crowd was a little different; quite a lot of older faces, and some familiar ones that hadn't been seen too much lately, I gathered; Petey Small, Jay Collins, Edgar Brown, all the people that Willie's blown down during the last month or so.

I have to hand it to Pitman, though, it was hardly a no-contest. Like a lot of other people there, I imagined that his European trip would have slowed him down a little, especially after playing with some of those rhythm sections, but he's a genuine giant, no question about it. The stuff comes steaming out in a torrent, and his control is really quite superlative, but the sheer power that he puts into it was what undid him tonight.

It was bull versus panther; direct energy spending itself against subtlety and fantastically judged pacing, and I guess the result was inevitable. Five hours of blowing the way Pitman did would have decimated a mastodon, and to be fair he hasn't had any real competition to speak of for the past year or so.

But even if he'd been physically up to it, I doubt that it would have ended any other way. The ragged edges were really beginning to show towards the finish—"Blue Lou" especially—and there's an element of frustration about his last few choruses. He played the last hour with his coat off and his shirt open right down to his trousers, and it was like a wet rag. Even his pants were soaked. By the time he quit, he was drained, blown out.

I can't find words for Willie right now. I've never really believed that it was possible for any of these people to actually produce the kind of sustained virtuoso performances that they were credited with, but at this particular point in time I have to accept that, on occasions at least, it did happen. He genuinely does seem to have no limits; not only that, his sense of form and continuity is absolutely incredible at this stage. One thing is becoming very obvious: "Willie's Blues" might have been the greatest thing he ever put on a commercial recording, but in fact he matched it time and again, and at far greater length.

He's still showing no real signs of wear, although the stories about his private doings are pretty hair-raising, some of those I've heard. I had a drink with him afterward, and I was amazed at his condition. He wasn't even sweating, and Pitman had gone out of there like a wet sponge. Every time we meet I expect him to mention "the other guy", but he never does. But he's still waiting for him, I can tell. He has that look in his eye, the one that says that there's still one more mountain out there somewhere, and he won't really feel that he's made it until he's stuck right up there at the top with no company in sight.

Pitman was a milestone, but to Willie he's still well short of the peak, and after tonight I guess he won't be alone in thinking that.

Thus are the mighty fallen, for the time being, at least. But Pitman's lucky, if only he knew it. Another twenty-six years for him, another fifteen months for Willie. It's a strange, hard world.

*Tuesday, June 14th, 1938*
*Room 88, Spicer's Hotel, New York*

A complication of a kind; not drastic, but it's something that I've been expecting for a long time, and I'm only surprised it didn't happen sooner.

He played a radio date with the band last night, and I met him afterward in a bar called Button's a place where musicians generally go after broadcasts. He had a cold, and he asked if he could come over here to put his feet up for an hour or so instead of going on to play somewhere. He said his throat was pretty sore, but he didn't want to go home just then.

Right off I had an idea of what he was really after, but there would have been no point in stalling. We came back here and had a couple of drinks and talked, and after a while he asked if I still had the gadget, as he called it.

I said that I didn't, that I was still having trouble with it and I'd left it back in Baltimore until I had a chance to really work on it, get it right before I tried to market it again.

He didn't like that. He stared at me, the kind of stare that suspects all kinds of nameless subterfuge but can't make up its mind exactly what it could be. I tried to get the conversation going again, but he didn't want to talk. He hadn't even wanted my company, and now that he'd failed to get what he came for he wasn't going through any more pretense that he did. He finished his drink without speaking, and said he was going. I said I hoped the cold would clear up soon, and that I'd be seeing him. He replied in just about as noncommittal a way as it's possible to without actually spitting in your eye, and went.

As I say, it wasn't too much of a surprise. He's been very withdrawn with me on my last couple of trips, and it isn't hard to see why. He thinks of me now as the one person who'll be able to say who's the original and who's the plagiarist when "the other guy" does eventually turn up! What a tangle. I suppose it's almost tragic in its way, but I must admit that it has its funny side as well.

It would be interesting to know just how closely he actually connects me with what's been happening to him, though. The fact of our always meeting at the really crucial times and in such widely spaced locales must have got him speculating by now, surely. He suspects something, but whether or not it goes beyond some kind of sleight-of-ear, for God only knows what bizarre purpose, I can't imagine. He certainly doesn't think I'm his fairy godmother, anyway.

Bad joke. Less than four weeks to go now. It's too bad about his cold, which is genuine enough. If he knew how precious time was to him, he'd have spent the whole evening blowing somewhere instead of wasting it on an abortive business like his call here.

For the thousandth time I'm almost tempted to shoot the works and tell him. Almost, but not quite. I stretched the rules once, but only because there was no other way. He's on his own, and that's how it'll have to stay.

*Friday, September 10th*
*2078 Lewiston, Maine*

It won't ever be possible to record this in a truly objective way, but I can't put it off forever. I suppose I've been hanging on to the hope that time would at least blunt the edges before I tackled it, but if it does then it's an imperceptibly slow process. It's been over two months now, and the details are still as sharp and clear as if it were only yesterday. Maybe this will help to clear my thinking, which is still very confused. It may even help me to find answers of a kind, although this seems less than a possibility at the moment.

I'll try to keep off the why's and wherefore's this time, too. I still can't make up my mind just how much sense my speculations on the first couple of threads made, if they made any at all. This thing is so complex that it only emphasizes our inability to understand even our own time and place, if such an expression means anything anymore. If only—

I'm getting bogged down already. Straight facts, in as far as that's going to be possible.

He still didn't look really sick during the last few days, not even particularly tired. I'd expected to find him showing real signs, but even after the marathon at the Joyland, when he took on all the big guns and shot them to pieces like a flock of sitting quail, he looked pretty much as he had ever since K.C.; a little more pouchy under the eyes, maybe, but nothing more.

But I was still of two minds how to wind things up. The actual product of the Consort session was on record, which was all that really counted, and the idea of actually witnessing his collapse had always been distasteful, really nothing more than an exercise in morbid curiosity that I'd already pretty well decided I could do without.

In the event, I went to West 44th Street on the evening of July 8th, stationed myself in a hamburger joint opposite the studios, and waited there: a half-hearted gesture of farewell, I admit, but one that I felt compelled to make. On the aural evidence he'd been in complete control at the session, and yet he'd died almost immediately afterward. So it was curiosity that pulled me there; really, a partial resurgence of the unhealthy inquisitiveness that I'd rejected earlier, but which I found didn't repel me in quite the same way in its modified form.

It was a long wait, almost an hour and a half. I got a couple of mildly curious looks from the counterman after a while, but every so often I bought a fresh coffee and carried on checking the traffic across the way while it gradually got dark outside. Cee Hall arrived first and unloaded his kit from a cab, and Charlie Williams turned up with his bass ten minutes or so afterward.

Willie and Lacey and a couple of girls arrived twenty minutes later, sharing a cab.

It wasn't really possible to gauge his complexion in that light, but if anything he looked more relaxed and cheerful than he normally did as he paid off the cab while Lacey and the girls went on inside.

He had good reason to be happy, I suppose; his first recordings under his own name, with just about the best supporting talent available, and he must have been particularly pleased about getting Lacey to duck his Swingtone contract and play the date. He always was the perfect accompanist for him, and they never jelled better than on the two tracks that they were going to cut that night.

I sat there for a minute or two after he'd gone into the studio, wondering about it, but more relieved at that moment than curious. It really did look as though it were going to be as clean as could be reasonably expected, which at least meant that there would be no gradual enfeebling decline to be borne and fretted over, the kind of ending that had no place in the existence of a comet as bright as he had been.

Cheered, in a bleak kind of way, I left and walked back to the hotel; a longish pull, but I wanted to take a final look at the town by night, because this was the place and the time that for me summed up most of the attractions of the era. But my principal feeling when I finally walked in off the street was one of relief.

I'd suddenly become obsessed with the idea that I had no right to be there at all; that despite the facts of history the setting and myself were two different kinds of incompatible shadow, intermingling only to the extent that oil and water do; touching at the surface, but nothing more. It's a contradiction, I know, but it was very real just then, and it has at least a suggestion of logic on its side.

Different kinds of experience and thought and feeling, all born of the circumstances of their time; how can such things ever do more than just show their skins to the stranger? The concept of such a fusion has an unreal quality about it, one that I somehow think I shall never be able to accept completely.

I settled my account with the usual excuse that I'd probably have to leave at very short notice in the morning, and went up to my room. I got rid of excess clothing down the laundry chute at the end of the corridor, packed, and put on the transfer suit.

As I checked and set the power packs on the suit and my case, I had this nagging thought that the thing was finishing all wrong; that a flat ending simply didn't fit in with the spirit of what had happened during the past few weeks. The dying fall is the right close to lots of encounters, but not this one, I was sure. It had been excitement and discovery right from the start, the kind of experience that demanded a statement summarizing all that was best in what I'd found.

I dug out the spool with "Willie's Blues" on it, fitted it, and ran it back to the programme number, put the recorder back in the case and switched to play. Then I activated both power packs, sat down on the edge of the bed, and listened.

It's music that I've heard God alone knows how many times, and it's one of the few pieces that has stood the test of frequent repetition, the only real test as far as I'm concerned. I must know every note, almost every nuance of what's played, and yet it always sounds as though it's being created right at the very moment of my listening to it. It's a genuine miracle of a kind, dovetailed so perfectly that there isn't a note or a beat that isn't an essential part of its structure. But it was sad music then, despite its buoyancy, because it was a requiem, shadowed by the things I knew about its creation.

I had my head lowered; so I didn't see the door open as they were working through the final bars. But then the latch clicked shut, and I looked up, and there he was, leaning against it and staring at me with wide, blank eyes. And then the music cut out, and the only sound in the room was his breathing; a ragged, grating, desperate noise that filled my head and choked off my own breath as if my heart had suddenly been grabbed by a huge, cold hand.

\* \* \* \*

I can't for the life of me imagine what he thought or felt at that God-awful moment. I can list my own reactions easily enough—disbelief, fear, and then pity and remorse when the truth of what must have happened and was happening right then hit me.

But as for him, I simply don't know, and his reading of the implications of what he saw is going to remain a mystery that I have no particular desire to solve.

How was it possible for me to have been so completely blind for so long? I've always thought of myself as a reasonably intelligent person, but intelligence is the ability to think past the surface of events and see the reality that lies underneath. I hadn't done this at all. I'd been too flattered by the importance of my role as catalyst to see that I wasn't simply showing him the road to tragically short-lived glory and enduring legend.

In effect, what I'd done was implant something in his mind; something that, when the time came for him to create that particular pattern of sound, would strike through him with all the awful force of an internal explosion, devastating his reason and triggering the physical disaster that his abuse of his body had already paved the way for.

The clues had all been there. The detailed reports of his death told how he'd recovered from the initial attack sufficiently to leave the building on his own, brushing aside all offers of help, and had finally been found in an alley an hour or so later, where he'd apparently collapsed for the last time. Remembering these things now was like the revelatory moments I'd experienced when we first met, the sudden flashes of insight that showed the puzzle neatly interlocking, a beautifully tooled exercise in cause and effect.

But until that moment I'd seen no link, no unifying thread to tie them all together and show the whole picture. Like any scavenger, or dumb, brainless bird, I'd seen only the bright side of the coin, all the time blind to the shadows on its reverse. But even when it isn't out in plain view, the balancing factor is never really absent, always there, always visible to eyes with thought and imagination behind them.

He was already far gone when he came into the room; wet, greying face, weak movements that he couldn't coordinate properly anymore.

Whatever it was he'd expected to find there, it couldn't have been what was actually waiting for him; a man dressed in a black, skin-tight suit, with a control-box of some kind strapped to his chest; a crazy, unbelievable portrait in smoke that was fading even as he watched it. It was like kicking a man who's already three-quarters of the way over a cliff edge, providing the final impetus to his fall. As I moved away, with everything breaking up into the extraordinary grained effect that occurs during the period of actual transfer, dots and flecks that dance and multiply and hurt your eyes, I saw him reach out a hand; whether to try to grab me and hold me there or to push me away I've never been able to decide.

He was posed like that, shrinking and dying and dissolving into a billion pieces when the blackout pulled me under.

He didn't actually die right then, not in the true physical sense. He must have had just enough strength left to scramble away from the nightmare, only to find himself in a dark, grimy place where he fell and escaped from it forever. But even without my unwitting final assistance, it would still have happened, not right then, but soon. He was sick, possibly without his even knowing it, and the way he pushed himself, squeezing life for all it was worth, meant that there was only one possible ending.

But what was he thinking while he ran? Even if he'd had the time or the strength to consider it rationally, did he have the kind of imagination that could link the pieces together and accept a proposition as farfetched as the truth would have seemed in his own time?

I can't imagine that he would, or could. I think he died frightened and confused, after suddenly finding himself in the middle of a situation that defied everything he knew and understood, destroyed by an assault on his mind and body that it had been impossible for him to anticipate or defend himself against. Poor Willie. It must have been a terrible moment for him there in the recording studio, when time suddenly overlapped and he found himself transmitting his contribution to the echoes that had stayed in his memory ever since his one hearing of them; recognizing them, knowing them to be impossible, but committed to their completion; sounds that came from the past but were being made in the present, originating there.

I killed him. I can say it now without actually flinching, externally at least; so perhaps I've found what I was hoping to find when I started this personally prescribed therapy. The images are still there, but I think they've lost a little of their sharpness now. I suppose it means that I've learned to accept what I've known all along but, because of my final role, just couldn't bring myself to acknowledge; that the pattern was set and that my own part in it was an immutable fact that all the cursing and railing and struggling in the world wouldn't have cancelled out.

It's a familiar pattern, too, on reflection—not exactly exclusive to people who hear unique sounds or possess unique vision or who mould language to suit the singular rhythms that fill their minds, but they seem to fit it more easily than most.

But how many of them, I wonder, have been directed by people like myself—wide-eyed, narrow-visioned trippers who blunder through time like clumsy children, totally unaware of the real effect that they are having on people and history? I daren't think of some of the possible implications, not even now.

But why *me?* Perhaps it's a kind of compensation for a total lack of creative talent, history's method of making the achievement a collective thing in an oblique and cruel kind of way. I'll just have to learn to be grateful for having been the chosen recipient of this particular apple with the shiny skin and the big dark worm inside, ignore the sugar content in my feelings and applaud the monstrous humour of the powers of creation with the wry detachment that I guess it deserves.

Not easy, but necessary, now. And I have a feeling it's something we're all going to have to learn.

# ATTACK OF THE HICCUPS

Mr. Randolph Fitch undoubtedly possessed all the physical attributes of a convivial member of society. He was large, fatly so, red-faced, and he smelt of beer.

But something had equally undoubtedly now served to evaporate this natural jollity. He slumped heavily in his chair on the far side of the desk, silent and morose.

Dr. Burgoyne surveyed him with the keen eye of the diagnostician, and classified him as Hallucinations, Alcoholically Induced.

"I see Things," Mr. Fitch muttered, twitching. Dr. Burgoyne smothered a self-congratulatory smirk. Mr. Fitch swallowed, rather untidily. "Orange Things."

"Orange?" Dr. Burgoyne said. "Indeed? A feature that differs somewhat from the common run in cases of this sort. The normal preference is for pink, green or purple." He smiled, kindly.

"Oh?" Mr. Fitch said. He swallowed and twitched, brightening momentarily. "You mean you get a lot of it?"

"Chiefly during the festive season," Dr. Burgoyne said, "but all-the-year-round cases are not unknown." He permitted himself a small chuckle.

"Oh," Mr. Fitch said. He fingered one of his chins nervously. "Do they get better?"

"That depends," Dr. Burgoyne said, "on their Strength Of Will. Alcohol is like many of our pleasanter facilities in this particular respect. Over-indulgence is the Enemy of Health, the ever-present—"

"Do they hiccup?" Mr. Fitch asked.

Dr. Burgoyne said, "I beg your pardon?" He hated being interrupted. "Do who what?"

"These other people," Mr. Fitch said. "Do they have to hiccup to see these Things, or are they there all the time?"

"Hiccupping, of course," Dr. Burgoyne said, drily, "is a frequent feature of such cases, but not normally regarded as an essential ingredient."

"And their Things are pink and green and purple, not orange?"

Dr. Burgoyne shifted in his chair, and contrived a patient smile.

"Normally, yes."

Mr. Fitch slumped further, pathetically.

"Then they're different."

"In colour, certainly." Dr. Burgoyne conceded. He wondered how long he was going to take to get rid of this confounded soak. He had a golfing appointment at three. "But I seriously doubt that such a discrepancy removes them altogether from the same general category." He concealed a yawn. "This question of hiccupping, now. Do I gather that these creatures only manifest themselves if your imbibing results in an attack of this kind?"

"Oh, no," Mr. Fitch said. "They just come when I hiccup."

Dr. Burgoyne frowned.

"You mean they appear during any glottal spasm, however caused?"

"Glottal—?" Mr. Fitch said, fogged.

Dr. Burgoyne ground his teeth quietly.

"Hiccupping," he said, "is the involuntary contraction of the diaphragm while the glottis is spasmodically closed. Hence, glottal. The causes are multiplicate, but generally—"

"Oh, I see," Mr. Fitch said. "Hiccupping. Yes, that's it. When I hiccup."

Dr. Burgoyne breathed heavily and ground a heel punishingly into the carpet beneath his desk.

"And of what approximate duration is their appearance at such times?"

Mr. Fitch selected another chin, fingered it, and continued to vibrate at short intervals.

"Well, that's the funny part. I can only see them at the top of the hiccup, so to speak."

"The top of the hiccup?"

"Well, you know how it is," Mr. Fitch said. He ceased his chin-massaging, and jerked his hand up and down. "When you hiccup, you sort of jerk."

Dr. Burgoyne stared.

"And it is only when you reach the apex of this movement that these creatures become visible?"

"That's it," Mr. Fitch said. He nodded eagerly, then immediately lapsed back to his former state of twitching lethargy. "That's when they're there, all right. Things like orange cactuses—you know, spikes, and so on—and they live on this plain where this mauve mossy stuff grows—"

"Mauve," Dr. Burgoyne said, "mossy stuff?" He felt a slight pounding in his temples. Really, some of these people possessed the most revolting outlandish sub-conscious. "A plain?"

"That's it," Mr. Fitch said. "And there's this sort of greeny-blue sky and everything— Well, anyway, when I went there first, nobody took any notice of me, didn't see me, I suppose. But they soon cottoned on all right, because every time I go back now, there they are in a big ring, all staring".

Dr. Burgoyne cleared his throat, rather tiredly.

"Staring? With what?"

Mr. Fitch was plainly puzzled by this question. "With what? Why, their eyes. Naturally".

"Of course," Dr. Burgoyne said. He punished the carpet with both heels and slowly and murderously cracked his knuckles. "Their eyes. Stupid of me."

"And they've started sort of leering, too. Well, anyway," Mr. Fitch said, "I started to get a bit scared and decided it was about time to get some help."

"Quite so," Dr. Burgoyne said. He glanced surreptitiously at his watch. "Very wise. Er—without going into any great detail, Mr. Fitch, when and how did these ah—creatures—first put in an appearance?"

Mr. Fitch produced a large handkerchief from a trouser pocket and removed a modicum of perspiration, pondering. "Well, it must have been about nine weeks ago, now, I suppose. Nine or ten."

"And did this initial encounter follow any form of excess on your part? A heavy meal, possibly an evening's drinking?"

"Why, no," Mr. Fitch said. "Nothing like that at all." He manipulated his handkerchief with a wobbling hand. "I was out walking the dog one evening, and it was my pipe that did it."

"Your pipe," Dr. Burgoyne repeated, a trifle dully.

"That's it," Mr. Fitch said. "Well, I must have let a bit of smoke leak down the wrong tube, or something, because I started coughing, and when I'd finished coughing I had the hiccups. And there they were," Mr. Fitch said, wetting his lips with a rather pale tongue, "all orange and spiky and all the rest of it."

"Quite so. And they have been visible during every subsequent bout of hiccupping, however caused?"

Mr. Fitch nodded his head, rapidly.

"That's right. All staring—"

"And, no doubt, leering," Dr. Burgoyne said. He wondered how the devil he could terminate the interview rapidly, short of kicking Mr. Fitch out. The man was obviously paranoiac to a degree—he brightened. Of course. "Well, Mr. Fitch, I must confess that your case contains some unusual features which I have no doubt would prove of extreme interest to certain colleagues of mine. Dr. Bush, I am sure, is far better equipped to advise on such—"

"But you don't understand," Mr. Fitch said. The frequency of his twitch had increased considerably, and despite his continuous working of the handkerchief, he now looked positively varnished. "I think they're up to something with this crane thing."

"Crane thing?" Dr. Burgoyne echoed. He sagged slightly. "I'm afraid—"

"I forgot to mention that bit," Mr. Fitch said. "They've just wheeled this sort of crane thing up, you see. It's got a big grab on it, and it sort of hums."

"Ah," Dr. Burgoyne said, hollowly.

"Well." Mr. Fitch said. "I can't see them going to all this trouble for nothing, can you? I mean, fetching a big clumsy thing like that, eh? It looks fishy to me." He smiled, feebly, and dabbed at his glossy forehead. "Can't help wondering if it's something to do with me being there."

Dr. Burgoyne stoically manoeuvred a smile into position. "But my dear chap, you're not actually going anywhere. Surely you must realise that these fig—"

"Well," Mr. Fitch said. He looked doubtful. "No, I suppose not, really." Dr. Burgoyne relaxed a little. Better, better. "After all," Mr. Fitch said, "it's only my head that keeps bobbing in and out."

"Your head?" Dr. Burgoyne said. He eyed Mr. Fitch's head, then his breadth of body and meaty hands, and experienced a distinct qualm. "Bobbing in and out?"

"Well, that's a bit of an exaggeration really." Mr. Fitch said, "It doesn't all go in, you see. It's only the top bit that vanishes".

"Ah? Indeed. Quite so," Dr. Burgoyne said. He fervently wished that Mr. Fitch would vanish wholesale. "It's not a common occurrence, exactly, but there is a great d—"

"Well, it stands to reason." Mr. Fitch said, reasonably. "I mean, it can't be here and there, can it? Anyway, I knew it felt as if it was popping off on its own account, so I said to my sister—I was round having tea at her place at the time—'Here, Freda,' I said, in between hiccups, that was. 'Watch my head a minute.' So she did," Mr. Fitch said, with due solemnity.

Dr. Burgoyne inclined his buzzing head and succeeded in raising his eyebrows.

"Well," Mr. Fitch said, gloomily. "That did it. She never was strong, wasn't Freda. She hollered out. "Randolph, where's the top of your head going to, oh Randolph, and that was it. Wallop," said Mr. Fitch, descriptively.

Dr. Burgoyne manfully attempted to continue his role of prompter through a mouthful of glue.

"Ah?" he said.

"God rest her." Mr. Fitch said, with heavy piety. "A good sister to me, she was. Paid for the funeral myself, of course. I mean I felt sort of responsible, after all."

"These hiccups, now," Dr. Burgoyne said glueily, eyeing the onyx penholder to his right. He wondered if it would be possible to stun Mr. Fitch with it should such an action become imperative. He persuaded his features to mould themselves into an expression of solicitous inquiry. "How frequently do they occur?"

"Well, that's just it," Mr. Fitch said. "They've been coming pretty regular over the last three weeks, and every time there's more of them".

"The attacks are increasing in duration and intensity?"

"Well, no, not really." Mr. Fitch said. "I mean there's more of these orange things."

"Ah," Dr. Burgoyne said. He fiddled with the lobe of his left ear. "Quite so. Well, Mr. Fitch, I can assure you that I will give this matter my most serious consid—"

He paused. Mr. Fitch was straightening in his chair in an oddly deliberate way. Dr. Burgoyne inched a coldly damp hand towards the pen-holder.

"I think," Mr. Fitch said, pressing one hand to his corpulent middle and the other to his mouth, "they're coming."

Dr. Burgoyne offered a brief prayer for this proffered straw, and rose gingerly.

"A glass of water," he said, and retired at speed to the adjoining bathroom.

He held a tumbler beneath the tap with a hand that shook, he noted irritably, considerably more than such absurd circumstances required. It was unpleasantly plain, of course, that the man was deranged, but to what degree... He turned off the tap, and thoughtfully filled a hypodermic with a slightly cloudy fluid.

There was a fearful shriek from the next room, inexplicably followed by a sound remarkably like that of a very large cork being removed from a very large bottle.

Hypodermic at the ready, Dr. Burgoyne inched cautiously to the doorway. He poked his head into the next room and stared.

Mr. Fitch was no longer visible. Above the vacant chair, in mid-air, was a mauve-fringed patch of greeny-blue. Through it, a loathsome apparition covered with spikes squirmed into view. It flopped to the carpet, then straightened. It was bright orange, and at least seven feet tall. It studied Dr. Burgoyne in a leeringly thoughtful sort of way, then advanced rapidly.

"You are a figment of Mr. Fitch's alcoholically over-stimulated sub-conscious," Dr. Burgoyne said, unhappily. "Go away".

The orange cactus thing ate him, fastidiously expectorating his hypodermic, fountain-pen, buttons, small change, and the metal parts of his suspenders as it did so.

# OUTSIDER

At first sighting. Marcus estimated that the pub was about three-quarters of a mile away, roughly equidistant from the hills that formed the flanks of the small valley in which it sat in shadowed isolation. He spotted it as they crested the southern range; a fairly substantial building, its details rapidly becoming obscured by the gathering dusk There was still sufficient daylight, though, to permit identification; the parking lot beside it, fronted by its supplementary sign, the garden and white tables at its rear.

Good timing, he thought, relieved. There was a chill in the air, and clouds were beginning to thicken darkly above the eastern horizon. Despite its bleakly inevitable lack of welcoming occupants, the pub still generated associations of warmth and relaxed conviviality, a friendly refuge. Some of its contents would probably prove to be distasteful, of course, they could be removed and evidence of their presence at least partially disguised. The smell of disinfectant was something that he accepted as an essential part of their world now.

They were roughly a third of the way down the gently coiling road when the light appeared, a small patch of brightness that winked into sudden existence at the side of the building facing their line of approach.

Marcus's first thought was that it was simply an open window catching the last rays of the almost vanished sun; a final trace of the dying day, briefly captured by the angle of the glass. But as remnants of daylight continued to fade and the sun finally slid below the curving line of the hills, the light grew brighter, a small, enigmatic rectangular beacon that gradually caused him to drift to a halt at the edge of the road.

The building was barely visible now, blurred to a misshapen shadow in the gloom, the light the only certain evidence of its location. He said, frowning, "There's someone down there. There's no other explanation." He bit his lip. "Is there?"

Paul said, "No. There's been no power of any kind for more than two months now. It's most probably an oil lamp. Whatever it is, somebody had to light it."

"What about an auxiliary generator?"

Paul shrugged. "Same thing. It would still need someone to operate it. And the light came on only a couple of minutes ago."

Marcus nodded, his initial sense of shock already subsiding. He knew that he could always rely on Paul to rationalize things, stay cool and un-flurried in the face of the unanticipated. Although he vaguely tended to think of himself as the leader of the trio, he relied on the strengths of the others to bolster his own impetuosity and fits of depression.

He'd often reflected that without them he very probably wouldn't have survived as long as he had. But Paul's steadiness and common sense and Alan's ability to detect the bizarre humour of their situation continued to hold at bay the despair that ceaselessly prowled around the perimeter of his consciousness.

"Female?" Alan speculated. "Tallish, but not exactly Amazonian, preferably blonde, in her late twenties? Attractive, of course, and an enterprising cook."

Marcus smiled. "And with the right sense of humour, of course."

"You mean she'd have to laugh at your jokes. Oh, essential."

Marcus continued to smile wryly. The chances of their meeting such an idealized companion were woefully improbable, of course. There had been women among the handful of survivors that they'd encountered since beginning the trek north, but none of them had remotely resembled Alan's flippantly sardonic specification.

A capacity for survival was all that mattered now, the ability to adapt, to manufacture and preserve some kind of tolerable existence in the aftermath of disaster.

He flexed his shoulders, easing the pressure of the pack and bedroll where they lay heavily across his back.

"Whoever it is, they have to be immune, I suppose. I wonder if there's more than one?"

Paul said, "There might be. There's no guarantee that they'll welcome strangers, either. Remember what's happened before. They might think that we're carriers. Better keep the gun handy."

Marcus nodded again, wriggled free of the pack, and took the gun from it. The metal felt hard and dependable against his hand. He un-zipped his jacket and wedged the gun behind his belt at his left side, its butt facing forward. He zippered his jacket again, then eased the pack back on. It was almost dark now, a moonless, cold evening with a touch of rawness in the air.

"Right, then. Let's see what we've got here."

An erratic breeze was funnelling through the valley as they reached level ground. The stench of manure could still be detected there, to some extent masking the other smells brought to them on the gusting wind.

At least the darkness hid the source, Marcus thought. He'd learned to detect the subtle differences by now, the somehow coarser pungency of animal decomposition as compared with its human counterpart. In his mind's eye he visualized the occupants of the surrounding fields; most of them, perhaps all, reduced to scattered mounds of putrefaction, their slow disintegration unaided by the traditional visitations of scavengers whose own ranks had been brutally decimated to a handful of cautiously selective survivors, instinctively mistrustful of infected flesh.

Animal and bird still bred, but it would be a long time before some semblance of normality returned to field and woodland and sky. Cities and towns, too, he supposed, although they didn't really matter anymore. Perhaps it will be their world now, he thought. Perhaps humankind will simply fade away, increasingly insulated from the possibility of continuity by its terror of contagion, ironically doomed to extinction by its capacity for reasoned fear.

There was some kind of vehicle parked in the shadows beside the pub. He saw its dully metallic glint as they passed the parking lot and approached the building, their footsteps muffled by the grass fringe beside the road.

The curve of the road had taken them some way to its right. From this adjusted angle of approach, Marcus saw that in fact three windows were illuminated; the one that they had first seen, located in the side of the building, and two others at its left front centre, previously hidden.

He could see the lighted room now bathed in the whitish glow of the lamp that sat on a table directly adjacent to the front corner window. At first no one was visible, then a shadow drifted across the far side of the room and a figure moved briefly into view before vanishing again, concealed by the corner wall.

A woman? The sighting had lasted no more than a second, but he'd caught a glimpse of what could have been long, dark hair. Meaningless, he told himself. His own hair was almost shoulder-length by now. The others maintained the same relatively neat styles that they'd affected throughout their acquaintance, a consistency of image that he found reassuring in a way but simultaneously interpreted as a silent reproof aimed at his own more casual attitude toward such things.

He frequently told himself that he ought to copy their example, despite there being little real point in such adherence to the old normality.

But that wasn't important just now. He hesitated, uncertain of their next move.

Paul whispered, "Better get a closer look. We can't really see enough from here."

They moved sideways, avoiding the pool of light, then toward the corner of the building. Marcus leaned against the wall, peering cautiously through the front corner window.

He was looking into what was plainly the barroom. The woman was seated on a barstool, her back toward them. She was fairly slim, the belted coat she was wearing shaped to contours confirming her gender. Black, slightly wavy hair hung loosely down her back and across her shoulders.

Her elbows were on the bartop, her hands hidden in front of her. Without being able to see them, Marcus guessed that she was holding a glass. As far as he could detect, there was no one else in the room.

He felt a tremor of unease. The tableau beyond the window had a bizarre, almost waxworks quality about it, he thought. It was like an almost too precise scene of another kind of reality that lived only in the memory: the clean, orderly setting warmed by the light of the lamp; the woman at the bar, the pose that she must have adopted at the moment of their arrival.

Perhaps she wasn't the one that he'd seen. There could be other people in there, undetectable from where he stood. He ducked down and moved along the wall to the farther window, but even this extension of his viewpoint failed to reveal anyone else in the room.

It was as though she was waiting for someone, he thought. He glanced uncertainly behind him, squinting into the surrounding gloom. Apart from the lighted windows, the darkness was almost total now, the only sound the occasional sigh of the wind as it brushed past the walls of the building.

Paul whispered, "Check around the side. We'll get a better view there."

They moved quietly around the corner, simultaneously stepping back several yards into the shadows beyond the throw of light.

Marcus stared through the side window, seeing the woman in profile now. This adjusted view appeared to confirm her solitude, but her face was indistinct, shadowed by the lamp behind her and partially masked by the curtain of hair. He could see the glass now, clasped between her hands where they rested on the bar; a tumbler, its dully amber contents almost reaching the brim.

They moved away from the window again, carefully circumnavigated the building, then returned to their starting point and conferred.

Despite the clement of unreality, it was cautiously accepted that there was no logical reason for supposing that the situation contained any kind of genuine risk. Their inspection of the rear and farther side of the premises had failed to find any other lighted windows or additional evidence of occupancy, so it seemed reasonable to assume that the woman was alone as she appeared to be.

And in the by now improbable event that she was a carrier, Paul pointed out, their own immunity had long proved itself to be an established fact.

But prudence would still be advisable. Marcus should go in alone while he and Alan remained hidden until the position became clear.

The woman's response to any new presence could range from terror to abject relief, and the arrival of an individual ostensibly posed less of a threat than that of a group.

Marcus allowed his initial reluctance to be overcome by this reasoned argument. Too, the wind had risen and was already cutting searchingly through his clothing. It would be a relief to be indoors, sheltered by the thick stone walls. He took a deep breath, and walked around the corner to the front of the building while the others melted into darkness.

The door creaked as he opened it, and the lamp flickered, its flame stirred by the inrush of air. The woman swung around, her face drawn and startled.

Marcus was disappointed to see that she was older than her rear view had led him to believe; certainly well past forty. It was a sallow, pouched face, patterned with fretful lines. She wore lipstick, dark against the pale skin.

They stared at one another for several seconds, Marcus politely guarded, the woman poised and wide-eyed. The glass in her hand slopped some of its contents onto the top of the bar, creating a slowly spreading pool.

"Don't be alarmed," Marcus said. He lifted a placating hand, pushing the door closed behind him. "There's nothing to be frightened of. I wasn't expecting to find anyone around here."

His voice sounded all right, he decided; calm and reassuring. He carefully shrugged out of his backpack and placed it on a bench beside him, conscious of the gun against his side.

He and the woman were the only people in the room, but a door beyond the end of the bar counter was open, leading into an unlit corridor. He stayed where he was, lifting both hands now. "There's nothing to worry about. Really."

The woman said, "Who are you?" Some of the shock was leaving her face, but her voice was thick with barely disguised tension. It was a north-country voice, heavily accented. Her back view really had been misleading, Marcus thought.

As well as being older than he'd anticipated, he'd somehow pictured someone less coarse-featured. She didn't look particularly intelligent, he decided. She could be a little drunk, too.

He kept his hands open and raised, carefully manufacturing a smile. "My name's Aitken. Marcus Aitken. I'm on my way up to Edinburgh. I have—" He corrected himself. "I had relatives there. I want to find out if any of them are still alive."

The woman said, after a pause, "I didn't hear any car."

Hadn't she made any kind of logical deduction regarding his backpack? Obviously not. Well, it confirmed his estimate of how bright she was. He continued to smile. "I'm walking. I never learned to drive."

"Are you on your own?"

He hesitated only fractionally before replying. Better not bring the others in just yet, he thought. She might accept their presence, even be relieved by the time-honoured concept of safety in numbers, but he couldn't be sure.

She could react with alarm, feel more threatened, and like some of the others that they'd met, be panicked into doing something foolish or dangerous. He had no way of knowing whether or not she carried any kind of weapon.

"Yes. There aren't many people left anywhere now. The ones I've met just seem to want to stay where they are."

Careful, he thought. That could be interpreted as a kind of criticism, potentially dangerous ground. "It's understandable, of course. They're used to being in certain places, that kind of thing." He shrugged and slowly brought his hands down.

"Look, there's no need to be frightened of me. All I want to do is sleep here tonight. Would you mind if I do that?"

She continued to stare at him, fixedly. Her eyes were no longer startled, but something else was growing there, a kind of hungry speculation.

She ignored his question. "I can drive. I've got a car outside. I could take you to Edinburgh."

This abrupt acceptance and invitation jarred him badly. *Damn,* he thought, dismayed. Perhaps he should have told her about the others straight away, after all. But it was always difficult to know what was best in such a situation.

Each stranger was an unknown quantity, an unpredictable and potentially risky intrusion into their world, and previous encounters had sometimes gone badly when their group presence had been realized.

I'd better not tell her just yet, he thought. Such an abrupt reversal of his claim to solitariness would be bound to invoke instant mistrust. He'd better establish some kind of relationship first, attempt to manufacture an area of common ground before tactfully revealing their presence.

But there was no question of her joining them, he thought. Apart from her age and appearance, he could sense the total absence of rapport between them. He'd learned to detect such things long ago, as far back as his early childhood, and his ensuing limited relationships had always been dictated by his instinct in such things. Their meeting could have spanned only a minute or two so far, but already he knew that she was a creature responsive to a different code of signals, the possessor of criteria alien to that of himself and the others.

He smiled again. "That's very kind of you." He looked around the bar. "Is this where you were living when it happened?"

She slowly shook her head. "I'm from Bolton."

"Did you know anybody here?"

She shook her head again. There was a shadow of colour in her face now. "No. I was just driving. I got here two days ago."

"Were there many survivors in Bolton?"

The colour went again, abruptly. Her face trembled, suddenly slack and lost. She began to cry.

He stayed where he was, further dismayed. He'd never been able to cope with tears and the appalling loss of control prompted by their activation. He thought briefly about his wife and their eventually disastrous relationship; the mutual death of understanding, punctuated by complaints and recriminations. And always tears. It's a weapon, really, he thought. They know we can't handle it when they cry.

He remained tactfully still and silent as the woman began to talk, her voice thick and halting at first but gradually resolving into a dull, hurting whine.

He listened to her catalogue of personal disaster with part of his mind, but principally was reflecting with relief on his own circumstances.

It was hard to see any really acceptable future, but compared with most of the people that he'd encountered since it had all happened, his luck had been incredible. Despite their tentative deductions, he still didn't know for sure why he and Paul and Alan should have remained immune, but the passage of time had established it as a fact, now proven beyond all doubt.

All around him, people had died; slow, suffering ends most of them, as the virus permeated their systems, first inducing fever, then dehydration and eventual death. His wife had been an early victim, a shock that had been smothered by the magnitude of what was happening everywhere.

For days he'd wandered the northern suburbs of London, desperately seeking familiar faces among the steadily dwindling handful of survivors that he found; some of them, like him, searching for family or friends or acquaintances, the majority locked away in what had become private fortresses against the unbelievable horror of it all, their presences betrayed only by a half-seen face at a window, an occasional moving curtain.

He'd been near total despair when Paul and Alan appeared. They'd arrived one evening, after he'd returned to the flat at the end of another fruitless day; an instinctive homing ritual, meaningless in itself, but one that could have meant their never locating each other if he had lapsed into the kind of rootless wandering practiced by some.

Their presence was like a sudden shaft of daylight entering his dark existence. Both unmarried, Paul and Alan had been on a walking tour of Wales when the virus swept like an unseen shadow across the country and the world. The holiday had been an annual get-together in which he normally joined, but pressure of work had made it impossible on that last occasion.

They'd spent a week, they told him, doing what they could for local victims before the scale of hopelessness of the task became evident. Then they had split up and gone to their parents' homes, but re-joined forces shortly afterward when the pointlessness of this filial loyalty had been proved. It was then that they decided to look for him in the all too probably vain hope that he, too, had somehow survived.

They'd laughed and talked, his own laughter near hysteria initially, but gradually subsiding to normality as he grew to accept the blessed fact of their re-union. They were both plainly shaken by their experience, but neither had really changed: Paul, fundamentally serious but with a dry, precisely worded sense of humour; Alan the extrovert, the compulsive conversationalist, the more overtly comic.

They'd gravitated toward each other during their college days; an unlikely alliance in some respects, but one that they collectively found pleasurable, and after graduating they'd made it a point to stay in touch over the intervening years.

Their survival, like his, remained unexplained, but a solitary clue had existed from the start. Both he and Paul had AB positive blood, an oddity that they'd learned during their last year in college after deciding that actual donation was the only way to overcome their mutual aversion to a form of public service that they found commendable. It had become something of a running joke that they periodically teased one another with; blood brothers, they'd called themselves. At the time Alan had been unable to overcome his own squeamishness, and his blood category remained unknown. Could he, too, belong to this same relatively rare group? They'd speculated endlessly on the freakishness of such a coincidence, the only straw of possibility that offered itself, while simultaneously accepting that explanations were of no real importance.

All that did matter, they'd agreed, was that they were together, sustaining each other through the nightmare, repelling it with their companionship and unwavering compatibility.

The woman's voice had levelled to a monotone now, heavy with exhaustion that was largely emotional. Eventually she stopped talking, the sound petering to silence. She stared past him, her face streaked and her eyes dull and blind.

She's talked herself out, he thought. Now would be the best time to tell her. He said gently, "It's a terrible thing, being alone, I know." He looked around the bar. "This is a nice place. I can see why you decided to stay here for a while."

He walked a little ways away from her, unzipping his coat and glancing at the empty tables and seats. He turned, spreading his hands. "Look, I must tell you. I didn't tell you before, because I thought you'd be more scared. I have two friends with me. We decided it would be best if they waited outside until I'd talked to you and made you realize that there wasn't anything to be frightened of. You aren't frightened anymore, are you?"

She didn't reply, simply stared blankly at him. Did she understand what he was saying? he wondered.

"I'll fetch them. It's getting pretty cold outside. They'll be glad to get indoors."

He went to the door, conscious of her eyes following his carefully unhurried movements. He opened it and looked out into the darkness. "It's all right. You can come in now."

They emerged out of the gloom and went past him into the bar. He shut the door and turned, gesturing introductions. "This is Paul, and this is Alan. We were friends at college. We still don't know why we all—" He stopped.

The woman left her stool and was stepping sideways through the open counterflap, her head turned in their direction, her eyes flickering restlessly. She reached below the counter, and the twin barrels of a shotgun appeared above its far edge.

He fumbled the gun from his belt and fired, crouching. His first shot missed, but the explosion and the shattering glass behind her panicked the woman into half turning away, her eyes squeezed closed. His second shot threw her against the rear wall, dislodging more bottles. She fell, disappearing beneath the counter. A brief silence was broken as another bottle slid free of its holder and dropped, making a soft, muffled sound on landing.

It must have fallen on her, he thought. He remained crouching, the gun stretched out in front of him, listening for any further sign of movement. There was no sound of any kind. Still pointing the gun, he went behind the counter. The woman lay on her stomach, her head twisted sideways in a reeking pool of spirits, the barrels of the shotgun projecting from beneath her body. He could see the bullet hole, a dark opening in the side of her head, partially concealed by strands of her hair.

He swallowed his revulsion and disappointment He hadn't wanted anything like this to happen, but already he was used to it in a way. People's responses had become increasingly irrational since the disaster. It could be just normal fear, he supposed, but alternatively it might mean that they hadn't fully escaped the effects of the virus after all. Perhaps some individuals had avoided death only to have their minds harmed in some way, a kind of insanity that was the price to be paid for staying alive.

Paul and Alan came out from where they'd taken shelter, and consoled him, pointing out that he'd had no choice. In fact, the shotgun, on inspection, turned out to be empty, but he'd had no way of knowing that.

They left the bar and went upstairs, relieved to find no other bodies and no lingering odour of decomposition. The beds were neatly made and rooms clean; evidence of some final gesture of refusal to accept the inevitability of a disordered end. He wondered where the people were who'd run the place, where exactly it was that they'd died. Not that it mattered, of course. Location was one of the least important aspects of death.

He slumped tiredly onto one of the beds, thinking about the woman. For a brief moment, just prior to their actual meeting, the possibility had existed that he and the others had found a companion to share the curtailments of their existence, to round out the question of human needs. But she hadn't been right, he knew. Instinct had told him of the absence of compatibility, that the kind of empathetic relationship that they sought had once again been no more than a dream.

He pulled the covers over him and drifted into sleep, lulled by the gusting wind outside the bedroom window.

On the following morning they breakfasted in the kitchen, augmenting their own supplies with the few edible items that they found. They briefly discussed the events of the evening, but it was generally agreed that there would be no point in burying the body. After all, she was simply one of countless millions, and what had happened had been unavoidable.

They left by the rear entrance and walked away from the building, heading toward the low range of hills on the far side of the valley. It was a bright, clear day, with a faint breeze the only reminder of the previous evening's sharp-edged wind.

It was a relief to be leaving there, Marcus thought. What had happened had been unfortunate, but in a way it had been for the best. The woman's frightening readiness to batten onto him, followed by her pathetic monologue and then the abrupt reversion to dangerous antagonism when the presence of the others had been made known had demonstrated her instability. Really, she was better off now, free of the ghosts that she endlessly mourned and no longer a threat to those like himself who had mercifully remained untouched by this appalling alternative to death.

And the truth, of course, was that she would never have fitted in; would always have been an unwanted intruder, a potentially destructive element that might ultimately have damaged the homogeneous balance of the group and the tolerable existence that they had created to insulate them from the ever-present nightmare.

He talked to Paul and Alan as he walked; a lone chattering figure, his solitary shadow darkening beside him as the sun rose and he began the climb that led out of the valley and toward the beckoning north.

# REASON

The perspective of the mind is a vulnerably flexible thing.

I realise that this isn't very subtle thinking and not even particularly well expressed, but I've never been forced to recognise its truth so clearly before. A man has died, and because of this and the things he said to me before he died, all the carefully selected blacks and whites that made up the majority of my opinions and beliefs have been suddenly and violently smudged to an unreadable, faceless grey.

Somewhere in that grey the truth is hiding. Why? Why does it hide? I still sense its presence, but I can't see its colour or the form it takes, and for the first time I feel a sense of reluctance in my own acceptance of the relationship that exists between us. Can this be right, chalo, this sudden wariness? I feel you now, applying your cooling compresses of reason to my fevered imagination, but there's a flaccidity, a lack of something—interest?—in your actions.

I'm afraid of you.

I might as well face up to that now. Fear, of course, breeds fear, and already I find it frightening that I should feel fear at all. Crazy thinking? How can it be? This is a world of sanity, where man and chalo have cast out the devils and tormentors and sweet reasonableness is king. But as I sit here, scribbling these notes in the gradually cooling greenness of my conservatory, the fear remains, and this provides me with a tangible of a kind, a dark starting-point where I can begin to at least try and grope my way out of the mist and re-arrange my thoughts into some sort of coherent order.

And although my conversion to a belief in the ultimate goodness of creation is a recent thing and possibly exempts me from the right to expect an answer to my prayers, God knows that it is for the sake of all men that I hope they make the same pattern as before…

* * * *

I first saw the man by the ornamental lake that occupies the centre of Willis Park. His back was towards me as I approached along the path that leads to it and then skirts its perimeter, and even though I couldn't see his face I could sense his indecision. It was in his stance the hunch of his shoulders, the oddly identifiable immobility that broadcasts acute uncertainty.

I walked past him, glancing casually as I did so. I caught a glimpse of a white, hard-fleshed face that carried a shadow of beard, and bright eyes that stared fixedly ahead, empty and unseeing.

At the time I felt only mild curiosity in the matter. He was simply an unshaven man, better-dressed than most unshaven men are, admittedly, who seemed to have a problem that was really none of my concern. I left the park and completed my errands, taking perhaps an hour. As soon as I re-entered by the south gate, taking my customary short-cut, I saw him again. He didn't appear to have moved at all, and although considerable distance separated us, I could still see the oddly bunched, spring-like tension of the way he stood facing the water, almost animal-like in its immediate connotations.

I was interested now. I walked at a pace quite suitable for a man of my years, ostensibly studying the surrounding flora, but watching him from the corner of an eye as I slowly approached where he stood.

My eyes have always retained their sharpness of focus, and from a distance of about fifteen yards I was able to study his face more closely. It was white, waxy, a sick face. Although I've been retired a little over three years now, I still retain the medical man's inability to curb my curiosity where these things are concerned. I moved a little closer and sat on a bench that faced the water, casually studying the swans that glided gently beyond the fringe of lily-pads.

Silent minutes passed. I fumbled my pipe from my pocket and sought methodically for matches, keeping my eyes on the slow, graceful activity of the birds. I sensed gradual movement from where he stood, but affected not to notice immediately. I tamped tobacco in the pipe bowl, went through the slow ritual of lighting it, and then allowed myself to glance in his direction.

His face shocked me. There was no pretence in his own pose; his eyes were fixed unblinkingly on me, with a curious look of appraisal in them. After a moment, I smiled, nodded, and turned my head away again, wondering briefly and uncomfortably if he was nothing more than a homosexual seeking his own kind, but there was a lack of sensuality about the planes of his face that seemed to classify this possibility as doubtful.

I tucked the matches away, wondering what to do. Should I speak? It would be simple enough to produce inanities about the state of the weather, or pretend to vaguely recognise him from some fictitious social affair, but perhaps it would be better to wait and see if his definite curiosity about myself was sufficient to induce him to make the initial approach.

Gravel crunched beside me, and I looked up to find him lowering himself slowly onto the far end of the bench.

For the first time I was able to study him in some detail. His general classification I found pretty straightforward; mid-forties, a higher-strata business type, tasteful but rather over-conservative dresser, that sort of thing. But there were flaws in the pattern. His nails were bitten to ugly, uneven travesties of what they must have once been, and the stubble on his chin was at least two days growth. But his eyes were the most disturbing feature about him. They were sick, but this was no malady in the medical sense of the word. This was the sickness of fear, the sickness of a mind that sees something dark encroaching on it and can find no escape.

His opening remark was delivered in an oddly colourless voice. He said, "You look like a sane man."

"We're all sane men," I said. I reached for the matches again, smiling, and trying to choose my words with care. "It's a sane world at last. Sane and safe."

"Safe," he said, and suddenly almost retched. He pushed a hand against his mouth, a sheen of sweat glistening on his face. His eyes closed, and he leaned slowly back against the seat, his hand still spread across his mouth.

I said, carefully, "Look, you don't seem to be any too well. Might I suggest you tell me what you think is wrong? I'm a doctor."

His eyes opened and slid sideways, displaying something that might have been slight curiosity. He said at last, almost inaudibly, "Cancer."

I felt a tug of pity.

"Is it inoperable?"

He breathed slowly and deeply, nodding his head.

"And there's no doubt at all that you have it?"

His sick, bright eyes rested on my face again.

"We all have it."

I stared at him for a long, silent moment, pulling on my pipe and floundering a long way out of my depth.

"What do you mean, exactly?"

He ignored the question, his eyes roaming restlessly across my face. Then he said, "What kind of doctor are you?"

"I'm retired, actually," I said. I felt vaguely and unnecessarily embarrassed. "I was a G.P. I sold my practice three years ago."

He nodded, disinterestedly.

"What do you know about the brain?"

I shook my head, slowly, still uncomfortable. "Not a great deal. That kind of thing is for the specialists. Do you have reason to believe that you have cancer of the brain?"

He said again, "We all have it."

I stared at him, suddenly understanding, a mixture of shock and terrible pity flooding through me.

"For God's sake, do you mean the Chalo?"

His face jerked to sudden life. Its planes altered subtly, frantic dartings of movement like the lightning passage of shadows flickering across its damp whiteness. His breathing was suddenly fast and shallow, and the sheen on his skin was very bright.

Then it was gone, and the haunted eyes were watching me from a face that was suddenly drawn and shrunken and very old. When he spoke, his voice was a dull, dead sound, almost devoid of inflection.

"You say you think it's a sane world at last; do you really believe that?"

"Of course I do."

"Because of the Chalo?"

"Yes," I said. "Of course. Without them—"

"What are they?"

I said, "I'm not quite sure that I—"

He was impatient, interrupting again with sudden, restless urgency.

"What are they? What are they, really? What do you, an educated, intelligent, thinking man, think they are?"

I said, slowly, "I think that they're what they say they are. The next stage in our evolutionary programme. Controlled energy of a very special nature that wanders through the universe in watch-dog packs, instinctively homing on species like ourselves who are at the end of their emotional tether and staying with them until insanity has been bred out of the genetic pattern." I looked at him, questioningly. "Do you have any particular reason to suppose differently?"

Again he abruptly veered onto a different conversational tack, ignoring my question.

"What were you doing when they came?"

I sucked on my pipe and thought.

"I was gardening," I said. The picture swam to the front of my mind and hardened into focus. "Cutting flowers, to be exact."

The faintest glimmer of a sick smile played on his face. "It was hot around here, wasn't it? Plenty of insects about, I expect."

I glanced at him. "Yes, there were."

"And you were finding them a nuisance." It was virtually a statement, not a surmise.

I nodded. "I was. But then I suddenly felt this coolness in my mind, this—calming freshness, I suppose you could call it, as if somebody—but, of course, you know."

His shudder was very real, and he moved his lowered head in jerking, nervous movements, as though seeking some misplaced thing. "I know."

"Then my own, personal chalo introduced itself," I said. I talked very calmly, watching the white, never-still face beside me. "It told of the countless billions of miles that it has travelled on its endless errand of mercy. It told of the other peopled worlds in our own galaxy and beyond, and the beings that inhabit them, some very much like ourselves, others vastly different. And it told of how many of these had had to be saved from themselves and their unbalanced technical and sociological achievements, and, like us, eventually made into complete, fully rational entities." I reached for my matches again. "An incredible record of good works, wouldn't you say?"

He was looking at me with a kind of exhausted curiosity.

"And you believe all this?"

I said, patiently, "In the eight months since they came, they've banished lunacy, war, and all their attendant evils. Suddenly, when we were so close to self-annihilation that it seemed utterly impossible to avoid it, we became sane." I stared at him. "You say we have cancer of the mind. We haven't, not now. It was the international disease before the Chalo came and did us the service of cutting out the rotten bit of our nature. Now, each man, woman, and child has the chain of its consciousness completed by a link that permits only rational thought and action. A man's chalo is the barrier between him and his old world of lunacy, unreasoning anger, and a million and one other signs of emotional immaturity." I struck a match and re-lit my pipe, surprised but pleased at my garrulity. Is this the sickness that you're afraid of? What kind of sickness is it that saves a world from its own inherent self-destructiveness?"

"And you find this an acceptable cure, despite its unnaturalness?"

"Unnatural?" I stared at him again. "But what could be more natural? What do we know about ourselves, let alone the rest of the universe? Now we've been granted a further glimpse of both. In my profession, before they came, it was sometimes incredibly hard to see any point in our being here at all, existing with senseless death and decay. It was one of the most difficult things in the world to believe in a God, other than one that epitomised futility. But the Chalo have done what no churchman ever did or could ever hope to do. By severing the channels of communication that translated unreason into action, they gave us the two things we needed most, hope and a future. And remember, nothing else was touched. Our natural traits of curiosity and ambition remain unimpaired—tempered by reason now, of course—which rather cancels out any accusations that might be levelled regarding the destruction of human initiative, and so on."

His sudden grin was a tight, bloodless affair, skull-like and entirely devoid of humour.

"What would you describe this as? An incredible exercise in selective lobotomy?"

"Miraculous," I said.

His eyebrows slid upwards, forcing dark lines of corrugation against his white forehead.

"But how do we know that it was?"

It had seemed that the conversation had at last reached something resembling firmer ground, but now I floundered again, unable to finger the relevance of his question. "I'm not sure—"

"Let me ask you again," he said. "What do you know about the brain? What do any of us know?"

I said, rather shortly, "Personally, very little, as I've already told you. Specialists know a great deal in some cases."

He grinned his death's-head grin again, and there was something derisive in it this time.

"Do you know how long it would take to map in full detail, one square inch of the surface of the cortex?"

I wasn't as surprised by the question as I perhaps might have been. Hypochondria often breeds its own illness, a rather unhealthy curiosity, and most libraries carry a basic selection of medical books.

I shook my head. "No, I don't."

"A quite incredible amount of time. So long, in fact, that only relatively few have been even roughly plotted." He was speaking in a more rational tone now, staring directly ahead across the faintly wind-rippled water of the lake, but it was a forced calm, induced by will-power and not peace of mind. "The brain is still a vast, unexplored continent as far as we're concerned, cluttered with so many points of intense interest that it's almost impossible to decide where to begin an investigation. And since we know so little about this all-important piece of ourselves, how do we know just what they've done to us?"

I said, "Because they've told us and it makes sense, surely."

"Does it?" His features were suddenly puckered as he stared at me. "We've been told that an incredibly clever piece of surgery has been performed on each of us, and we've believed it, unquestioningly. Why this eager, ready acceptance of the first explanation that's offered when there's an alternative that's just as logical? There's a simpler answer to that. Surgery generally means the permanent removal of whatever ails you. It's a far more comforting thought to assume that the evil has been cut out and cast away, rather than consider the temporary alleviation that could be provided by sedation of some kind." His expression was one of growing anger.

I nodded, slowly.

"And so the possibility that drugs and not surgery have been used has been comfortingly ignored or pushed into one of the dark, forgotten attics of our minds. Forgotten by all but a few, that is. Not the people with the best minds, perhaps, but the ones with the most inquisitive." He smiled, a sudden, rather ferocious and ugly smile. "It's an uncomfortable thing to live with, inquisitiveness. It nags, like a discontented tenant that you can't throw out, and it has an inevitable off-shoot. The hypothesis, another fascinating but prickly fellow to have around. He has innumerable variations, but like so many works of the imagination he eventually worms his way pretty close to the truth at times. And when he does, you know it."

The glisten of sweat was back on his face, and hysteria was gradually fighting its way through. I was bewildered and confused. In all my years as a medical man I had never felt so ineffectual, so completely at a loss. This was a man filled with illogical, twisted fear, the paranoiac nightmares of the demented, yet he lived in a world where such darkness no longer existed. I could almost see the struggle that raged behind the wet, shaking mask of composure. It was anger versus fear, the age-old battle between pride and panic, magnified now to frightening proportions.

I cleared my throat, and said, "And you think you've discovered another, altogether different reason for the presence of the Chalo?"

He nodded, a sharp, fierce jerk of his head.

"What is it?"

He said, hoarsely, "Listen to the ravings of a madman in a sane world. See what you say to my hypothesis, my little work of lunatic fiction." I watched his hands. They were grasping at one another, never still, like white, perspiring wrestlers seeking vainly for a hold. "Somewhere on another world, life evolves. It reaches intelligence, and eventually, when such a feat is technically feasible, and for one of a dozen possible reasons, it moves out into space, taking with it a formidable natural weapon. In the course of its evolution it's developed one of two things, both very alien to our own pattern. Either symbiosis is involved, or it's an entity capable of thought projection, which can enter and study the minds of others with which it comes into contact."

"You mean telepathy?"

He shook his head, violently.

"No. This goes beyond that, but it still has its limitations. It can exercise some control over the mind that it infiltrates, but when it comes up against intelligence above a certain level its hold is relatively slight. So, to handle such contingencies, it evolves a strategy, a long-term method of attack that is subtle and utterly invincible. It carefully selects certain items, the communicatory fibres that lead from the mind and activate the excessive physical responses to anger, insanity, and all the traditionally black segments of sensory reaction. Then it blocks them."

I said, fumblingly, "Blocks—?"

"It seals them off. With drugs, or more likely, some form of mental block that it can induce. It seals them so that no trickle of sensation can pass through, no irrational action can be sparked into being. Then it introduces itself to the race that has become its chosen victim, tells its meticulously conceived and quite plausible story, and is received with paeans of thanksgiving. Then it waits." Fear and fury were thickening his voice, clogging the wild flow of his words.

"It waits, while foolishly joyful people put their world in order for the very first time, destroying the arsenals and their world-poisoning contents. And while it waits, all the countless minor irritations that clutter day to day existence go on, the yelling children, the too-loud radio next door, the clumsy housewife and her never-ending crockery bills, the dog that leaves its hairs on the best upholstery, cold food that should have been hot, burned toast, traffic-jams—" He paused, breathless for the first time. "All registering as sight, sound, feel, or taste. Registering, and being recorded."

For the first time I felt the cold, probing fingers of doubt that fumbled at my mind, trailing a confusion of shadows behind them. As I watched the twisting, furious face that talked on beside me, I seemed to be catching sudden, frightening glimpses of sanity behind its sweat-streaked contortions.

"Minute, infinitesimal things in themselves, like the blows of a feather. And gradually the silt builds up, pushing against the barriers that have been erected in their natural outlets. No safety-valve remains open, no brief, cleansing spasm of temper is permitted. And then, when the good, rational things have been done, the poison of ultimate war neutralised and the arsenals replaced by buildings that house only the sane, humane activities of mankind, they withdraw."

I said in a thin, foolish voice that was a devitalized mockery of my own, "You mean they—leave?"

Suddenly, he crumbled. It was a horrible thing to see. His face, already ashen, became a soaking rag of dead flesh that twitched uncontrollably. The anger was gone, seared out of existence by the fear that tore at him unopposed now. And with it, something else had gone. His eyes were an animal's eyes, wide, wild, and almost empty. He tried to speak, but all that came was a rasping, muffled sound, utterly devoid of intelligibility.

Then he was gone, lurching up from the bench and across the close-cropped grass towards the boundary of the park. I heard fading sounds as he ran, choking, animal-like noises that lashed at my consciousness. I pushed myself to my feet, shouting after him, but there was no pause in his grotesquely clumsy progress.

I looked desperately around. Two women with prams had broken off their conversation and were staring as he blundered past them. No one else was in sight. I started to run, but no man of sixty-seven is equipped for such demanding activity. My breath was gone almost immediately, but I stumbled on, my mind a sluggish, groping blur, and my legs automatically jerking forward and back, forward and back, like two rusted, unwilling pistons.

I'd covered barely twenty yards when he reached the gate and vanished. There was a lapse of perhaps three or four seconds, then the bitter squeal of tyres sounded suddenly from the road outside. I jolted to a stop, breath suspended, hearing, almost feeling the faint thud, followed instantly by the grinding crash of metal on stone.

I moved on again, but slowly now. My heart was nearly pushing its way through my chest, and I felt desperately sick with the certainty of what I would find.

He was a crumpled, boneless heap on the far side of the road. Just beyond him a van was wedged drunkenly across the pavement, its nose half-buried in a sagging brick wall. As I passed through the gate, its off-side door squealed protestingly open and a man almost fell through it. He was holding his head with one hand and cursing wildly.

A knot of white-faced people were gathering. I walked through them, forced myself to my knees beside the still bundle, and pushed my hand beneath his jacket. There was nothing. No movement at all, no faint stirring that would have meant hope, however small.

I crouched there, looking down at the twisted face that carried its own strange look of peace now, the confusion thickening darkly in my mind.

* * * *

I was still kneeling by him when the police and ambulance came. The two women who had been in the park were present at the front of the crowd then, staring at me with poorly veiled suspicion and occasionally turning sharply and whispering to one another. A constable questioned me, then a sergeant that I knew slightly. I told them both the same story, aware of the women's sharp-eared attention, watching their faces soften gradually to near-belief of what I was saying. I told them that he was a stranger to me, a seemingly sick man that I'd offered to help and who had confided his fears that he had cancer. Suddenly, in the middle of his tirade, he had simply bolted in a seemingly uncontrolled panic, raced into the road, and been unavoidably hit by the van.

The van driver, his head bandaged by the ambulance people, interrupted at this point. He said that the accident *had* been avoidable, not by himself, but by the dead man. He claimed that he had run head-on at the approaching van, as though it was a deliberately death-seeking action on his part. Two people in the crowd corroborated this, and the sergeant observed, with professional off-handedness, that the chain of incidents seemed to tie together logically enough and that the post-mortem would soon confirm or deny the presence of cancer and any justification, legal or otherwise, for the act.

The body, when searched, provided no means of immediate identification, but his raincoat yielded a laundry mark that could be investigated. The sergeant asked me if I knew his name, or recognised him from any past occasion. I said no. Then, as he put away his notebook, he asked me what I thought personally about the likelihood of cancer. Had I, as a doctor, detected anything in his reasoning to think that his suspicions about himself were grounded in fact?

I watched two black-uniformed men, brusquely efficient in their actions, slide the blanket-covered stretcher into the interior of the ambulance. They closed the doors, conferred briefly with the constable, climbed into the driving cab, and moved off. I watched them go, my eyes trying to pierce the metal of the doors, the fibre of the blanket, and then the flesh and bone that hid the now-dead truth, trying, trying…

Well, asked the sergeant, a little impatiently, had I?

I said I didn't know.

* * * *

And I still don't know. Now, as I sit in the darkening conservatory of my home, surrounded by the green comfort of my plants, my vines and shrubs, I'm trying desperately to find the answer to his question.

But am I? Do I really wish to uncover the truth behind the strange and terrible babblings that I heard only a few hours ago? For another strangely shocking thing has happened, perhaps the one thing more than any other that has created genuine doubt in my mind.

The police have identified the body, and it belongs to Kenneth George Butler, a consultant surgeon at the Longhurst Institute at Leeds, who disappeared from his home three days ago. This man, a specialist in the workings of the brain, called me an intelligent, thinking person, and, God help me, I suppose I am. Our conversation was an unfinished thing in the true sense, and its termination in violent tragedy, coupled with the knowledge of his identity, has left a fearful, prickling curiosity in my mind.

A part, at least, of what he said was true. How could we have been so blind? Perhaps we deliberately shut out the possibility that drugs and not surgery were the means by which we have been made into a reasoning, rational people, as he said we have done. Perhaps centuries of fear, of growing insecurity and doubts about our ultimate survival as a race ensured that we closed our minds against such a relatively unsatisfactory solution, and grasped eagerly at the first proffered explanation. Before commencing these notes, I read a book. It isn't a new book, and far more definitive documents on its subjects have been written since, but it's the only one I have. It has reminded me of many half-forgotten things and told me some that I never consciously knew. It tells of a man called Penfield and his early experiments with the epileptics in his care, how stimulation of their temporal lobes induced remarkable feats of memory. It reminded me of the hypothalamus, the small, vital knot of tissue at the base of the brain-stem that triggers the actions that satiate our wants and desires. In my own mind these things are now inextricably tangled, completing a strangely ominous pattern.

For these, and perhaps other strange weapons unknown to us yet, could transform the wild imaginings of paranoia into possibilities. With them, it would be possible to pervert what men of medicine, men of mercy have done, and spur this black and evil sediment, if it exists, into blind, senseless action, scattering its shards of indiscriminating destruction and ensuring rapid, total victory. For a brief while the gates of hell would open here on Earth, and we would be helpless, mewling children, less than children, less than the beasts of the field and forest, wreaking mindless vengeance on each other, unleashing the torrent of our vindictiveness against ourselves and bringing the hard-won world of man thundering down around us.

Is this what you have planned, chalo, you and your kind? Are you the Devil and not the God that mankind thinks it has found at last? Did this tortured man open a door and show me the ultimate darkness that you have hidden there, a world that will murder itself, but still remain a place where others can live? Are you what he thought you were, only segments of viscious beings that wait in the patient darkness, waiting until you have done your work and then drawing you back to themselves to wait a little longer while we, the suddenly mindless, do what remains to be done?

I'm very tired now, and very frightened. If I'm wrong to question your intentions, as he did, then you must try to forgive me. But a possibility can be a terrible thing, and these things are at least possible. We know so little about the universe, this vast, endless cave of mystery that contains us, that such happenings may be merely inexplicable parts of the scheme of things.

But for the first time, I am glad that I am old. I've lived a full life in the small part of the world that I chose, and whatever else should happen, it can't be long before it's over. But the world is full of youth and hope, and it's these things that I find myself sorrowing for. Does this mean that I've found my answer, chalo? Perhaps, but I still don't really know.

The sun has gone at last, and shadows fill my glass-walled room and the world outside. Around me, the green things sink into unstirring sleep, retreating from the chill of night that creeps across my drying bones like an icy shroud, drawn by strange, invisible fingers.

Darkness is almost here...

# ABOUT ROBERT J. TILLEY

The author was born in Cottingham, Yorkshire, 12th May, 1928. His father was a sales rep for National Cash Registers, and his mother a housewife. His family moved to Devon when he was four years old and three years later to Bridgwater in Somerset, where he grew up.

Tilley recalls: "Dad occasionally wrote poetry—not bad, some of it—and late in life Mum became a pretty good Sunday painter, so I obviously owe my creative streak to both of them.

"When I was small, my sister, who's eighteen months older, used to read stories to me, but because she was a bit hesitant and I was impatient to know what happened next I learned to read before I started school. I've been a pretty voracious reader for most of my life as well as a keen cinema-goer and jazz enthusiast, my love for which is reflected in a fair bit of my writing. I bought my first instrument, a clarinet, when I was sixteen and working as an auctioneer's clerk—a job for which I was totally unsuited—and later a tenor saxophone. I organised and played in various bands up to my mid-sixties when I had to pack it in because of health problems. Still tinkle on the piano and occasionally the vibraphone when I have the time and energy, which isn't often.

"I took a commercial art course at Bristol College of Art And Design in the late 1940's and after leaving worked initially as a screen printer. Subsequently worked as a graphic designer, specialising in display and exhibitions, and spent the final decade of my working life as a lecturer at a Further Education college in London, taking early retirement and returning to Bristol in 1985.

"My wife and I now live in the beautiful and blessedly peaceful Mendip hills, coping as well as we can with the infirmities and general drawbacks of old

"I followed what seems to be the commonplace route to an appreciation of science fiction; Flash Gordon serials at the local Saturday morning matinees when I was young, and I remember being very taken with the BBC radio serialisation of War of the Worlds, which used Holt's Mars, the god of war as its opening and closing music. Powerful stuff. I read Wells and Verne and occasional sf stories in magazines like Argosy, but the range of my early reading was quite wide—still is—and I only discovered the SF magazines when I was in "Once I got started, though, I couldn't get enough of it. I bought all the current magazines and pretty quickly decided to have a go myself; *Ellery Queen's Mystery Magazine* bought my first effort, a fantasy piece, and I broke into SF with a couple of sales to *Authentic Science Fiction*, just prior to its unfortunate demise.

"My subsequent early stories appeared in other British magazines such as *New Worlds*, *Science Fantasy* and *Nebula*. But when the home market sagged, I tried the USA, and was gratified to sell several stories to *Fantasy & Science Fiction*, some of which were later anthologized.

"My output has been sporadic to say the least—twenty-some stories and two novels over a sixty year period could hardly be described as prolific. I'm both astounded and impressed by the sheer volume and, generally speaking, consistency of work produced by people as diverse as Ballard and Tubb, but there's no way that I could have followed their industrious example.

"Writing was their vocation, but my butterfly mind has meant that I've only ever been able to concentrate on it in relatively short bursts. Variety is the spice of life, it's said, but while I've derived a lot of pleasure from my assorted activities I have to confess that ultimately, of all my creative efforts, writing has given me the deepest satisfaction."

www.ingramcontent.com/pod-product-compliance
Lightning Source LLC
Chambersburg PA
CBHW020656180626
46816CB00003B/1305